Season's Regency Greetings

Season's Regency Greetings

Two Christmas Novellas

Carla Kelly

Seattle, WA

Camel Press
PO Box 70515
Seattle, WA 98127

For more information go to: www.camelpress.com
www.carlakellyauthor.com

Cover design by Sabrina Sun

ISBN: 978-1-60381-254-2 (Trade Paper)
ISBN: 978-1-60381-255-9 (eBook)

Library of Congress Control Number: 2014955979
Printed in the United States of America

To all of my readers who love the magic of the
holiday season, whether it be
Christmas, Hanukkah, or Kwaanza.

∽

Books by Carla Kelly
Fiction

Daughter of Fortune
Summer Campaign
Miss Chartley's Guided Tour
Marian's Christmas Wish
Mrs. McVinnie's London Season
Libby's London Merchant
Miss Grimsley's Oxford Career
Miss Billings Treads the Boards
Mrs. Drew Plays Her Hand
Reforming Lord Ragsdale
Miss Whittier Makes a List
The Lady's Companion
With This Ring
Miss Milton Speaks Her Mind
One Good Turn
The Wedding Journey
Here's to the Ladies: Stories of the Frontier Army
Beau Crusoe
Marrying the Captain
The Surgeon's Lady
Marrying the Royal Marine
The Admiral's Penniless Bride
Borrowed Light
Enduring Light
Coming Home for Christmas: The Holiday Stories
Marriage of Mercy
My Loving Vigil Keeping
Her Hesitant Heart
Safe Passage
The Double Cross
The Wedding Ring Quest
Marco and the Devil's Bargain
Softly Falling

Non-Fiction

On the Upper Missouri: The Journal of Rudolph Friedrich Kurz (editor)
Louis Dace Letellier: Adventures on the Upper Missouri (editor)
Fort Buford: Sentinel at the Confluence
Stop Me If You've Read This One

Let Nothing You Dismay

⸻

IT WAS OBVIOUS TO Lord Trevor Chase, his solicitor, and their clerk that all the other legal minds at Lincoln's Inn had been celebrating the approach of Christmas for some hours. The early closing of King's Bench, Common Pleas, Chancery Court, and Magistrate's Court until the break of the new year was the signal for general merrymaking among the legal houses lining Chancery Lane. He had already sent his clerk home with a hefty bonus and a bottle of brandy from his stash.

Trevor had never felt inclined to celebrate the year's cases, won or lost. He seldom triumphed at court because his clients were generally all guilty. True, their crimes were among the more petty in English law, but English law always came down hard against miscreants who meddled with another's property, be it land, gold bullion, a loaf of bread, or a pot of porridge. A good day for Lord Trevor was one where he wheedled a reprieve from the drop and saw his client transported to Australia instead. He knew that most Englishmen in 1810 would not consider enforced passage to the Antipodes any sort of victory. Because of this, a celebration, even for the birth of Christ, always felt vaguely hypocritical to him. Besides that, he knew his solicitor was in a hurry to be on his way to Tunbridge Wells.

But not without a protestation, because the solicitor, an earnest young man, name of George Dawkins, was almost as devoted to his young charges as he was. "Trevor, you know it is my turn to take that deposition," the good man said, even as he pulled on his coat and looked about for his hat. "And when was the last time you spent more than a day or two home at Chase Hall?"

"You, sir, have a family," Trevor reminded him firmly. "And a wife eager to see her parents in Kent."

Dawkins must have been thinking about the events of last Christmas. "Yes, but I could return for the deposition. I would rather not ..." he paused, his embarrassment obvious.

"... leave me alone here, eh? Is that it?" Trevor finished his solicitor's thought.

The man knew better than to bamboozle. "Yes, that's it. I don't want to return to .... Well, you know. You were damned lucky last time."

Not lucky, Trevor thought. I thought I was home free. Damn those interfering barristers in the next chamber. "I suppose. I suppose," he said. "I promise to be good this year."

His solicitor went so far as to take his arm. "You'll do nothing besides take that deposition? You'll give me no cause for alarm?"

"Certainly not," Trevor lied. He shrugged off his solicitor's arm (even as he was touched by his concern), and pulled on his overcoat. He looked around the chamber, and put on his hat. Nothing here would he miss.

He and his solicitor went downstairs together and stood at the Chancery Lane entrance to the Inn. He looked up at the evening sky—surprisingly clear for London in winter—and observed the stars. "A rare sight, Dawkins," he said to his employee.

As they both looked upward, a little shard of light seemed

to separate itself from a larger brightness, rather like shavings from some celestial woodcarver. Enchanted, he watched as it dropped quickly, blazed briefly, then puffed out.

Dawkins chuckled. "We should each make a wish, Trevor," he said, amusement high in his voice. "Me, I wish I could be more than five minutes on our way and not have one of my children ask, 'How much farther, Papa?'" He turned to Trevor. "What do you wish?"

"I don't hold with wishing on stars," he replied.

"Not even Christmas stars?"

"Especially not those."

But he did. Long after his solicitor had bade him good night and happy Christmas, and was whistling his way down the lane, Trevor stood there, hesitating like a fool, and unable to stop from staring into the heavens. He closed his eyes.

"I wish, I wish someone would help me."

"MISS AMBROSE, DO YOU think we will arrive in time for me to prevent my sister from making this Tragic Mistake that will blight her life and doom her to misery? I *wish* the coachman would pick up speed!"

Cecilia Ambrose—luckily for her—had been hiding behind a good book when her pupil burst out with that bit of moral indignation. She raised the book a little higher to make sure that Lady Lucinda Chase would not see her smile.

"My dear Lady Lucinda, I have not met her, but from what I know of your family, I suspect she is in control of her situation. Is it not possible that your sister welcomes her coming nuptials? Stranger things have happened."

Her young pupil rolled her eyes tragically, and pressed the back of her hand to her cheek. "Miss Ambrose, in her last letter to me she actually admitted that Sir Lysander kissed her! Can you imagine anything more distasteful? Oh, woe!"

Cecilia abandoned her attempt at solemnity, put down the book after marking her place, and laughed. When she could speak, she did so in rounder tones. "My dear little scholar, I think you are lacing this up a bit tight. If the wicked stage were not such a pit of evil and degradation, you would probably be anointed a worthy successor to Siddons! It is, um, possible that your sister doesn't consider kissing to be distasteful. You might even be inclined to try it yourself someday."

The look of horror that Lucinda Chase cast in her direction assured Cecilia that the time was not quite ripe for such a radical comment. And just as well, she thought as she put her arm around her twelve-year-old charge. "It is merely a suggestion, my dear. Perhaps when you are eighteen, you will feel that way, too." It seemed the teacherly thing to say, especially for someone into her fifth year as instructor of drawing and pianoforte at Miss Dupree's Select Academy for Young Ladies.

Her young charge was silent for a long moment. She sighed. "Miss Ambrose, I suppose you are right. I do not know that Janet would listen to me, anyway. Since her come out she has changed, and it makes me a little sad."

Ah, the crux of the matter, Cecilia thought as the post chaise bowled along toward York. She remembered Miss Dupree's admonition about maintaining a firm separation between teacher and pupil and—not for the first time—discarded it without a qualm. She touched Lucy's cheek. "You're concerned, aren't you, that Janet is going to grow up and leave you behind?" she asked, her voice soft. "Oh, my dear, she will not! You will always be sisters, and someday you, too, will understand what is going on with her right now. Do trust me on this. Perhaps things are not as bad as you think."

Her conclusion was firm, and precisely in keeping with her profession. Lucy sighed again, but to Cecilia's ears, always quite in tune with the nuances of the young, it was not a despairing sigh.

"Very well, Miss Ambrose," her charge said. "I will trust you. But it makes me sad," she added. She looked up at her teacher.

"Do you think I will survive the ordeal of this most trying age?"

Cecilia laughed out loud. "Wherever did you hear that phrase?"

It was Lucy's turn to grin. "I overheard Miss Dupree talking to my mama, last time she visited."

"You will survive," Cecilia assured her. "I mean, I did." Lucy stared at her. "Really, Lucy, I *was* young once!"

"Oh! I didn't mean that you are precisely old, Miss Ambrose," Lucy burst out. "It's just that I didn't …." Her voice trailed away, but she tried to recover. "I don't know what I meant."

I do, Cecilia thought. Don't worry, my dear. You're not the first, and probably not the last. She smiled at her charge to put her at ease, and returned to her book. Lucy settled down quietly and soon slept. Cecilia put the book down then and glanced out the window on the snowy day. She could see her reflection in the glass. Not for the first time, she wondered what other people thought when they looked at her.

She knew she was nice-looking, and that her figure was trim. In Egypt, where her foster parents had labored for many years—Papa studying ancient Coptic Christian texts, and Mama doing good in many venues—her appearance excited no interest. In England, she was an exotic, Egyptian-looking. Or as her dear foster brother liked to tease her, "Ceely the Gift of the Nile." Cecilia looked at Lucinda again and smiled. And heaven knows I am old, in the bargain, she thought, all of eight and twenty. I doubt Lucinda knows which is worst.

She knew that her foster brother would find this exchange amusing, and she resolved to write him that night, when they stopped. It was her turn to sigh, knowing that a letter to William would languish three months in the hold of an East India merchant vessel bound for Calcutta, where he labored as a missionary with his parents now, who had been forced to abandon Egypt when Napoleon decided to invade. She looked out the window at the bare branches, wishing that her dear ones were not all so far away, especially at Christmas.

She had been quite content at the thought of spending Christmas in Bath at the Select Academy. Miss Dupree was engaged to visit her family in London, and the other teachers had made similar arrangements. She had remained at the Academy last year, and found the solitude to her liking, except for Christmas Day. Except for that one day, when it was too quiet, it was the perfect time to catch up on reading, grade papers, take walks without students tagging along, and write letters. That one day she had stood at the window, wanting to graft herself onto families hurrying to dinner engagements or visiting relatives. But the feeling passed, and soon the pupils and teachers returned.

Lady Maria Chase, Marchioness of Falstoke, had written to Cecilia a month ago, asking if she could escort Lucinda home to Chase Hall, on the great plain of York. *I cannot depend upon my brother-in-law, Lord Trevor Chase, to escort her because that dear man is woefully ramshackle. Do help us out, Miss Ambrose,* she had written.

At the time, Cecilia saw no reason to decline the invitation, which came with instructions about securing a post chaise, and the list of which inns would be expecting them. Miss Dupree had raised her eyebrows over the choice of inns, commenting that Cecilia would be in the lap of luxury, something out of the ordinary for a teacher, even a good one at a choice school. "I doubt you will suffer from damp sheets or underdone beef," had been her comment.

No, she did not wish to visit in Yorkshire. Lucinda had not meant to be rude, but there it was. I *am* different here in England, Cecilia thought. I might make my hosts uncomfortable. As they traveled over good roads and under a cold but bright sky, Cecilia resolved to remain at Chase Hall only long enough to express her concerns to her pupil's mother, and catch a mail coach south. It was too much to consider that the marquis would furnish her with a post chaise for the return trip.

Always observant of her students, especially the more

promising ones, Cecilia had watched Lucy mope her way through the fall term. Her pupil, a budding artist, completed the required sketches and watercolors, but without enthusiasm. As she gave the matter serious consideration, Cecilia thought that the bloom left the rose with the letter from home in which Janet announced her engagement to Sir Lysander Polk of the Northumberland Polks, a dour collection of thin-lipped landowners—according to Lucinda, who already had an artist's eye for caricature—who had somehow begotten a thoroughly charming son. Not only was Lysander charming; he was handsome in the extreme, and rich enough in the bargain to make Lord Falstoke, a careful parent, smile. Or so Lucy had declared, when she shared the letter with Cecilia.

The actualities were confirmed a short time later, when Lord and Lady Falstoke and the betrothed pair stopped at the Select Academy on their way to London's modistes, cobblers, and milliners. On acquaintance with Sir Lysander, who did prove to be charming and handsome, Cecilia began to see the difficulty. She watched how Lady Janet hung on his every word, and found herself unable to tear herself from his side during the entire evening. Cecilia could not overlook the fact that the more Janet clung, the quieter Lucinda became.

Cecilia looked down at her sleeping charge. It *is* a most trying age, my dear, she thought. Hopefully a visit home would prove the antidote. At least Cecilia could lay the matter before Lady Falstoke, and get help from that quarter.

They arrived at Falstoke in the middle of the next afternoon, and the view, even in December, did not disappoint. Cecilia listened with a smile on her face as Lucy, more excited as the miles passed, pointed out favorite places. Her smile deepened as Lucy took hold of her arm and leaned forward.

"Oh, Miss Ambrose, just around this bend!"

She knew that Hugo Chase, Marquis of Falstoke, was a wealthy man, but the estate that met her eyes surprised her a little. Chase Hall was smaller than she would have imagined, but discreet, tasteful, and totally in harmony with the setting of trees, meadow, and stream. She could see a small lake in the near distance.

"Oh, Lucinda!" she exclaimed.

"I love coming home," her pupil said softly.

They traveled the tree-lined lane to the circle drive and wide front steps, Lucy on the edge of the seat. When they came to a stop, Lucy remained where she was. "This is strange," she murmured. "No one is here to meet us." She frowned. "Usually the servants are lined up and Mama and Papa are standing on the steps." She took Cecilia's hand. "Can something be wrong?"

"Oh, surely not," Cecilia replied. "We would have heard." But we've been on the road, she added silently to herself. "Let us go inside." She patted Lucy's hand. "My dear, it is Christmastime and everyone is busy!" She saw the door open. "There, now. Uh, is that your butler? He is somewhat casual, is he not?"

Lucy looked up, her eyes even wider. "Something has happened! It is my uncle Trevor."

The man came down the steps as Lucy came up, and caught her in his arms. Cecilia was relieved to see the smile on his face; surely that did not signal bad news. It was a nice smile, she decided, even if the man behind it was as casually dressed as an out of work road mender. She couldn't really tell his age. She assumed that Lord Falstoke was in his middling forties. This uncle of Lucy's had to be a younger brother. How curious then, for his hair was already gray. She smiled to herself. And had not seen a comb or brush yet that day, even though it was late afternoon.

He was a tall man who, despite his disheveled appearance, managed to look quite graceful, even as he hugged his niece, then kissed the top of her head. No, graceful was not the precise word, she decided. He is dignified. I doubt anyone ever argues with him. I know I would not.

She left the post chaise herself, content to stand on the

lowest step quite unnoticed, as a young boy hurtled out of the open door and into his sister's arms. The three of them—niece, nephew, and uncle—stood on the steps with their arms around one another. She came closer, feeling almost shy, and Lucy remembered her manners. "Miss Ambrose, I am sorry! Allow me … this is my uncle, Trevor Chase, Papa's only brother. Uncle, this is my teacher, Miss Cecilia Ambrose."

Cecilia didn't see how he did it, not with children on both sides of him, but he managed an elegant bow. You are well trained enough, she thought as she curtsied back, even if you do look like a refugee from Bedlam. "Delighted to meet you," she said.

"I doubt it," he replied, and there was no mistaking the good humor in his wonderful voice. "You are probably wondering what lunatic asylum I escaped from."

It was not the comment she expected, and certainly not the appraisal she was used to: one glance, and then another, when the person did not think she was looking. Cecilia could see nothing but goodwill on his face, rather than suspicion.

"My uncle is a barrister," the young boy said. He tugged on the man's sleeve. "I shall go find Janet," he said, and went into the house.

"You are … you are a barrister?" she asked. The name was familiar to her. Was he a father of a student in her advanced watercolor class? No, that was not it. It will come to me, she thought.

"Miss Ambrose, he is the best barrister in the City," Lucinda assured her. She leaned against him, and Cecilia could tell that in the short space of a few minutes, all of Miss Dupree's deportment lessons had flown away on little wings. "Papa says he likes to right wrongs, and that is why he almost never comes here. There are more wrongs in London, apparently."

The man laughed. "You're too polite, dear Lucy," he replied, and gave his niece a squeeze before he released her. "He refers

to me as the patron saint of lost causes." He gestured toward
Cecilia. "Come indoors, Miss Ambrose. You're looking a little
chilly."

The foyer was as beautiful as she had thought it would be,
soft color on the walls, delicate plasterwork above, and intricate
parquetry underfoot. "What a wonderful place," she said.

"It is, indeed," Lord Trevor agreed. "I know there are many
country seats larger than this one, but none more lovely, to my
way of thinking." He rubbed his hands and looked around. "I
love to come home, now and then."

"Where is Mama?" Lucy asked as a footman silently
approached and divested her of her traveling cloak.

"Lucy! Thank God you have come! This family is beset with
Trying Events!"

Well, I suppose I can safely say that others in this family
besides Lucy tend to speak in capital letters, Cecilia thought
as she allowed Lord Trevor to help in the removal of her
cloak. Lucy ran to her sister Janet, who stood with her arms
outstretched dramatically.

"I do believe the most trying event is Janet's propensity to
be Yorkshire's premier actress of melodrama and melancholy,"
Lord Trevor murmured to her as he handed her cloak to the
footman. "I have only been here three days myself, and already
I want to strangle her."

She looked at him in surprise, then put her lips together so
she would not laugh.

Lord Trevor only grinned at her, which made the matter
worse. "Such forbearance, Miss Ambrose," he said. "You have
my permission to laugh! If you can withstand this, then you
must be the lady who teaches deportment at Miss Dupree's
Whatchamacallit."

"Far from it," she replied. "I teach drawing and the
pianoforte."

He took her arm through his and walked her down the hall
toward the two young ladies. "My dear Janet, wouldn't this

be a good time to tell your sister what is going on, before she thinks that pirates from the Barbary Coast have abducted your parents?"

"Lucy would never think such a thing!" Janet declared, looking at him earnestly. "I doubt there have ever been any pirates in Yorkshire."

Lord Trevor only sighed. Forcing down her laughter, Cecilia spoke up in what she hoped were her best educator's tones. "Lady Janet, perhaps you can tell us where your parents are? Your sister is concerned."

Janet looked at her, a tragic expression on her lovely face. "Oh, Miss … Miss Ambrose, is it? My parents have bravely gone into a charnel house of pestilence and disease."

Lord Trevor glowered at his older niece. "Cut line, Janet," he said. He put his arm around Lucy. "Amelia's brood came down with the measles three days ago, and your parents have gone to York to help. I expect them home tomorrow. Amelia is the oldest of my nieces," he explained to Cecilia over his shoulder. "It's just the dratted measles."

"Only this afternoon I wrote to my dear Lysander, who will drop everything to hurry to this beleaguered household and give us the benefit of his wisdom," Janet said.

"Janet, we can depend upon Uncle Trevor to look out for us," Lucy said shyly.

"Uncle Trevor is far too busy to worry about us, Lucy," her sister replied, dismissing her sister with a wave of her handkerchief. "And didn't he say over breakfast this morning that he must return to London immediately after our parents are restored to us? Depend upon it; Lysander will hurry to my side, and all will be well." She nodded to Cecilia. "Come, Lucinda. I have much to tell you about my dear Lysander."

"But shouldn't I show Miss Ambrose to her room?" Lucy asked.

"That is what servants are for, Lucy. Come along."

After a backward glance at Cecilia, Lucinda trailed upstairs after her sister. Cecilia's face burned with the snub. Lord Trevor regarded her with sympathy.

"What do you say, Miss Ambrose? Should we wait until Lysander arrives, tie him up with Janet, and throw them both in the river? It's too late to drown them at birth. Ah, that is better," he said when she laughed. "Do excuse my niece's manners. If I ever fall in love—and the prospect seems remote—I promise not to be so rude." He indicated the sitting room, with its open door and fire crackling in the grate. "Come sit down, and let me take a moment to reassure you that we are not all denatured, drooling simpletons."

She needed no proof of that, but was happy to accompany him into the sitting room. He saw that she was seated close to the fire, a hassock under her feet, and then spoke to the footman.

"Tea or coffee, Miss Ambrose?" he asked. "I know coffee isn't ordinarily served in the afternoon, but I am partial to it, and don't have a second's patience with what I should and should not do."

"Coffee, if you please," she answered, amused out of her embarrassment. She removed her gloves, and fluffed her hair, trapped too long by her bonnet.

The footman left, and Lord Trevor stood by the fireplace. She regarded him with some interest, because she remembered now who he was. Miss Dupree, considered a radical by some, subscribed to two London newspapers, even going so far as to encourage her employees to read them. The other female teachers seldom ventured beyond the first page. The Select Academy's two male instructors read the papers during the day while they drank tea between classes. When class was over, and if the downstairs maid hadn't made her circuit, Cecilia gathered up the papers from the commons room. She took them to her room to pore over in the evening hours, after she had finished grading papers, and when it was not her turn to be on duty in the sitting room when the young ladies were allowed visitors.

She knew next to nothing of the British criminal trial system, but could not resist reading about the cases that even Mrs. Dupree, for all her radical views, must have considered sordid and sensational. No matter; Cecilia read the papers, and here was a barrister well known to her from criminal trials, written up in the florid style of the London dailies.

I should say nothing, she told herself as she sat with her hands folded politely, her ankles together. He will think I am vulgar. Besides, I am leaving as soon as I can.

He cleared his throat and she looked up.

"Miss Ambrose, I am sorry for this disorder in which you find us."

He *is* self-conscious about this, she thought. I think he even wishes he had combed his hair. Look how he is running his fingers through it. She smiled. I suppose even brilliant barristers sometimes are caught up short. Well, join the human race, sir.

"Oh, please don't apologize, Lord Trevor," she said. She hesitated, then gave herself a mental shrug. This is a man I do admire, she thought. What can it hurt if I say something? I will be gone tomorrow. "Lord Trevor, I ... I sometimes read in the newspaper of your legal work."

"What?"

She winced inwardly. How could one man invest so much weight in a single word? Was this part of his training? Oh, Lord, I am glad I will never, ever have to face this man in the docket, she thought. Or over a breakfast table.

She opened her eyes wider, wondering at the origin of that impish thought. She reminded herself that she was a teacher, and dedicated to the edification of her pupils. Breakfast table, indeed! She dared to glance at him, and saw, to her temporary relief at least, he had not turned from the fireplace, where he warmed his hands.

"I beg your pardon, Miss Ambrose," he was saying, "I must have misheard. Do forgive me. Did you say that you *read the newspaper*?"

"I do," she replied simply. She discovered that she could no more lie to this man than sprout wings and fly across the plain of York. In for a penny, she thought grimly. "And ... and I am a great admirer of your work."

It must have been the wrong thing to say, she decided. Why on earth did I admit that I read the paper? she asked herself in misery as he slowly turned around from his hand warming. As he raised his eyebrows, she wished she could vanish without a trace and suddenly materialize in her Bath sitting room, grading papers and waiting for the dinner bell. "Well, I am," she said.

He smiled at her. "Why, thank you, Miss Ambrose." He seated himself beside her. "Do you pass on what you learn to your students?"

She listened hard for any sarcasm in his voice, but she could detect none. She also did not see any disparagement or condescension in his face, which gave her heart. "No, I don't pass it on," she said quietly, then took a deep breath. "I only wish that I could." She sat a little straighter then, suddenly feeling herself very much the child of crusading evangelists. "I believe you should receive great credit for what you do, rather than derision, Lord Trevor. Didn't I read only last week that you had been denied a position of Master of the Bench at Lincoln's Inn?"

"You did, indeed," he replied. "Sometimes I imagine that the Benchers wish I had been called from another Inn." He shrugged. "Even my brother Hugo calls this my 'deranged hobby.'"

The maid came in with coffee, which Cecilia poured. "You are going back to London tomorrow?" she asked.

"I am, as soon as Hugo and Maria arrive. Lowly Magistrate's Court does not sit during the holiday, but I have depositions to take." He took a sip and then sat back. "I know my solicitor could do that, but he wanted to spend the week with his family in Kent. I am, as you might suppose, a soft touch for a bare pleading."

"I am delighted to have met you, Lord Trevor," she told him.

The housekeeper stood at the door to the sitting room. Lord Trevor rose, cup in hand, and indicated that Cecilia follow her. "She'll show you to your room. We keep country hours here, so we will eat in an hour." He winked at the housekeeper, who blushed, but made no attempt to hide the smile in her eyes. "As you can also imagine, there's no need to dress up!"

Smiling now, the housekeeper led her upstairs. "He's a great one, is Lord Trevor," she said to Cecilia. "We only wish he came around more often."

"I suppose he is quite busy in London," Cecilia said. "Indeed he is," the woman replied, "even though I sometimes wonder at the low company he keeps." She stopped then, remembering her position. "Miss Ambrose, your pupil is across the hall. You'll hear the bell for dinner."

Cecilia decided before dinner that it would be easy to make her excuses the next day when Lord and Lady Falstoke returned, and take the mail coach back to Bath. She would express her concerns about Lucy to the marchioness before she left.

To her consternation, David looked as glum as his sister when he came into the dining room with Lord Trevor, who carried a letter. The man seated himself and looked at his nieces. "I received a post not twenty minutes ago from your parents," he said.

"They're not coming home tomorrow," David said. He looked down at his plate.

"Why ever not?" Janet asked, indignant. "Don't they know we need them? I mean, really, they took Chambliss with them, and Cook!"

"Chambliss is our butler," Lucy whispered to Cecilia.

"It seems that your older sister needs them more," Lord Trevor replied, his voice firm. "Do have a little compassion, Janet. They have promised to be here for Christmas. I'll be staying until they return."

Janet turned stricken eyes upon her uncle. "But they are to host Lysander!"

"Perhaps the earth will continue to orbit the sun if he has to postpone his arrival for a few days," Lord Trevor remarked dryly. "David, eat your soup."

They ate in silence, Lord Trevor obviously reviewing in his mind how this news would change his own plans. Cecilia glanced at Lucy, who whispered, "I will hardly have any time to be with her, before we must return to Bath."

"Then the time will be all the more precious, when it comes, my dear," Cecilia said, thinking of her dear ones in India.

David began to cry. Head down, he tried to choke back his tears, but they flowed anyway. Lord Trevor looked at him in dismay, then at Cecilia. As sorry as she felt for the little boy, she almost smiled at the desperation on the barrister's face. You can argue cases for the lowliest in the dockets, she thought, but your nephew's tears are another matter. She rose from the table. I have absolutely nothing to lose here, she thought. No one should be crying at Christmastime.

She walked over to David's chair and knelt at his side. "This is difficult, isn't it?" she asked him quietly. "I know your mama wishes she were here, too."

"She's only twenty miles away!" Lord Trevor exclaimed, exasperated.

"It's a long way, when you're only—are you six, my dear?" she asked the little boy, who had stopped crying to listen to her. She handed him her napkin.

"Seven," he mumbled into the cloth. "I am small for my age."

"You know, perhaps we could go belowstairs and ask the cook for …."

"Mama never coddles him like that," Janet said.

"I would," Cecilia answered. She looked at Lord Trevor, who was watching her with a smile of appreciation. "Do you mind, sir?"

"I don't mind at all," he replied. "Miss Ambrose, do as you see fit."

Cecilia took David downstairs. The second cook beamed at the boy, and suggested a bowl of the rabbit fricassee left from luncheon. In another minute, he was eating. Cecilia sat beside him, and Cook placed a bowl of stew before her, too. "If you don't mind leftovers," he said in apology. "I know Lord Trevor don't mind, but there are them above stairs who are a little too high in the instep these days."

"Janet makes us eat in the dining room," David said when he stopped to wipe his mouth. "We always eat in the breakfast room when Mama is here." He glared at the ceiling. "*She* thinks it is not grand enough."

"I think Janet is going through a trying time," Cecilia said, attempting to keep her face serious.

He shook his head. "Grown-ups do not have trying times."

They do, she thought. "Perhaps now and then."

She sat there, content in her surroundings, as David finished the stew. He pushed away the bowl when the cook brought in a tray of gingersnaps with a flourish, and remembered his manners to offer her one.

"Any left for me?"

You're a quiet man, Cecilia thought as she looked over to see Lord Trevor standing beside his nephew. David made room for his uncle on the bench. He passed the biscuits, even as the cook set a glass of milk in front of Lord Trevor. He dipped a biscuit in the milk and ate it, then looked at her. "Try it, Miss Ambrose. Anyone who reads newspapers can't mind dipping gingersnaps."

"Will I never be able to live that down?" she said as she dipped a gingersnap.

He touched David's shoulder. "It is safe to go above stairs now. Your sisters have retired to their room, where Janet, I fear, will continue to brag about darling Lysander."

"Oh, dear," Cecilia murmured. "I have to speak to Lady Falstoke about that."

"Then you must remain here through the week," Lord Trevor told her.

"I couldn't possibly do that," she replied as he gestured for her to proceed them up the stairs. "I will write her a letter from Bath."

The three of them walked down the hall together, uncle and nephew hand in hand. They paused at the foot of the stairs. "David and I will say good night here," Lord Trevor told her. "I brought my files with me from Lincoln's Inn, and he is helping arrange my 1808 cases alphabetically."

"But it is 1810," she reminded him. "Nearly 1811."

"I'm behind." He ran his long fingers through his hair, a gesture she was coming to recognize. "Not all of us were kissed by the fairy of efficiency at birth, madam!"

She laughed, enjoying that visual picture. He smiled at her, then spoke to David, who went on down the hall.

"I can't get you to change your mind?" he asked, keeping his voice down. "You can see from my ham handling of David at the dinner table that I need help." He hesitated. "I seldom stay here until Christmas. Well, I never do."

"I am certain you will manage until your brother and sister-in-law return." Cecilia curtsied to him. "Thank you, Lord Trevor, for your hospitality. If you can arrange for a gig to take me tomorrow to the mail coach stop, I will be on my way to Bath."

He bowed. "Stubborn woman," he scolded. "What is the big attraction in Bath?"

There is no big attraction in Bath, she thought. "I .... It's where I live."

He took her hand. "That is almost as illogical as some of the courtroom arguments I must endure! Good night, Miss Ambrose. We will see you on your way to Bath tomorrow, since you are determined to abandon us."

"You are as dramatic as your nieces," she chided him.

"I know," he said cheerfully. "Ain't it a shame?"

SHE WASN'T CERTAIN WHAT woke her, hours later. Her first inclination was to roll over and go back to sleep. All was quiet. She sat up and allowed her eyes to focus on the gloom around her. Nothing. She debated whether to get up and look in the hall, but decided against it. That would mean searching for her robe, which she hadn't bothered to unpack, considering the brevity of her visit.

Then she heard it: someone pounding up the stairs and banging on a door down the hall. She leaped out of bed, ran to her door, and opened it at the same time she smelled smoke. Her hand to her throat now, she stepped into the hall. She thought she recognized the footman, even though he was wearing his nightshirt. "My lord! My lord!" he yelled as he banged on the door.

The door opened, and Lord Trevor stepped barefoot into the hall. "Fire, my lord," the footman said, breathless from dashing up the stairs. "The central chimney!"

Cecilia hurried back into her room, grabbed her traveling case, and threw it out the window. She snatched her cloak, stepped into her shoes, and turned around to see Lord Trevor right behind her. He grabbed her arm and pulled her into the hall. "Stay here," he ordered. "You don't know this manor." Smoke wafted up the stairs like her vision of the last plague of Egypt. She pulled a corner of her cloak across her face to cover her nose, and watched Lord Trevor go in the bedchambers and awaken his nieces and nephew.

He pulled David out first, and thrust him at her. She locked her arms tight around the sleepy child. "We'll wait right here for your uncle," she whispered into his hair.

Lucinda came next, her eyes wide with fear, and Janet followed, wailing about her clothes. "Shut up, Janet," her uncle ordered. "Take Lucy's hand and hold mine."

With his free hand he grabbed Cecilia around the waist and started down the stairs. David coughed and tried to pull away, but she clutched his hand. She put her other arm around Lord Trevor and turned her face into his nightshirt so she could breathe. No one said anything as they groped down the stairs and across the foyer. In another blessed moment the footman, who must have been in front of them in the smoky darkness, flung open the front door. They hurried down the steps into the cold.

Still he did not release her. She kept her face tight against his chest, shivering from fright. If anything, he tightened his grip on her until his fingers were digging into the flesh of her waist. He must have realized then what he was doing, because he opened his hand, even though he did not let go of her.

She forced herself to remain calm, if not for herself, then for the children, and perhaps for Lord Trevor, who surely had more to do now than hold her so tight on the front lawn. She released her grip on his waist then, and stepped back slightly, so he had no choice but to let go.

Before he did, he leaned forward and kissed the top of her head. Because he offered no explanation for his curious act, and no apology, she decided that emergencies did strange things to people who were otherwise rational.

"Keep everyone here, Cecilia. No one goes back for anything." He turned and hurried up the steps again.

What about you? she wanted to call after him as he disappeared inside. She gathered his nieces and nephew around her. "We'll be fine, my dears," she told them, reaching out her arms to embrace them all. They stood together and watched the manor. Although smoke seeped from the front door, she saw no flames.

They endured several more minutes of discomfort, then Lord Trevor and the household staff came around the building from the back. The footman, more dignified with trousers now, carried the grip she had thrown out the window. Lord

LET NOTHING YOU DISMAY   21

Trevor had also taken the time to find his own pants and shoes, although he still wore his nightshirt. To her amusement, the housekeeper was fully dressed. *I'll wager you would rather have burned to a crisp before leaving your room in a state of semi-dress*, she thought.

Lord Trevor hurried to her, the housekeeper and footman following. "Mrs. Grey will escort you and the children to the dower house for the night. It's in that little copse."

"Can you save our home, Uncle?" Janet asked, clutching his arm.

He kissed her cheek. "I rather think so. The servants are inside the kitchen now, where the fire appears to have originated. We'll know more in the morning, when it's light." He looked over Janet's shoulder at Cecilia. "If you can keep things organized, I'll be forever in your debt."

They followed Mrs. Grey to the dower house, which she hadn't even noticed yesterday when they arrived at Chase Hall. All the furniture was shrouded in holland covers, which made David cling even tighter to her. He relaxed a little when the footman flung away the covers, and then dumped coal in the grates and started fires.

She decided that the dower house gave new meaning to the word cozy. A trip upstairs revealed only two bedchambers, one with a small dressing room. Since it was so late, Cecilia directed Mrs. Grey to pull out blankets. "I think proper sheets and coverlets can wait for morning," she explained as she handed each girl a blanket. "You girls take the chamber with the dressing room, and I will put David in the other one. Come, Davy," she said, resting her hand on his shoulder, "I think that you and your uncle will have to share."

"He snores."

Cecilia laughed. "Then you will have to get to sleep before he does, won't you?"

Below stairs, Mrs. Grey had already made room for herself. "I'll send the footman to the manor for food, and you'll have a good breakfast in the morning," she assured Cecilia. "Where are you planning to sleep, Miss Ambrose?"

She took the blanket Mrs. Grey held out. "I will wait up for Lord Trevor in the sitting room. Perhaps tomorrow we can find a cot for the dressing room." She looked around, already anticipating a busy day of cleaning ahead. If Janet keeps busy, she won't have time to complain, Cecilia thought. If Lucinda keeps busy with her sister, they might even remember all those things they have in common. If Davy keeps busy, he won't have so much time to miss his mother. She wrapped the blanket around her shoulders, savoring the heavy warmth. She thought at first that she might sit up on the sofa, but surely it wouldn't hurt to lie down just until Lord Trevor returned. She closed her eyes.

WHEN SHE WOKE, THE room was full of light. Lord Trevor sat in the chair across from her. She sat up quickly, then tugged the blanket down around her bare feet.

"I thought about covering them, but reckoned that would wake you." He coughed. "Lord, no wonder chimney sweeps seldom live past fifteen," he said when he finished coughing into his handkerchief that was already quite black.

"Let me get you something to drink," she told him, acutely aware that she was still in her nightgown, her favorite flannel monstrosity that was thin from washing.

"Mrs. Grey is bringing in coffee, and probably her latest harangue about the way I take care of myself." He sighed, then gave her a rueful look. "Lord spare us from lifelong retainers, Miss Ambrose! They must be worse than nagging wives."

She laughed, and pulled the blanket around her shoulders. If ever a man looked exhausted, she thought, it is you. He was filthy, too, his nightshirt gray with grime, and his hair black. Bloodshot eyes looked back at her. When he smiled, his teeth were a contrast in his face.

He held up his hand. "No harangue from you, Miss Ambrose, if you please."

"I wouldn't dream of it," she replied serenely. "I don't know you well enough to nag you." She paused and thought a moment. "And even if I did know you better, I do not think I would scold."

"Then you are rare, indeed."

She shook her head. "Just practical, sir! Don't we all pursue our own course, no matter what people who care about us say?"

She could tell that her words startled him; they startled her. "I mean …." she began, then stopped. "No, that was exactly what I meant. Anyone who does what you do in London's courts doesn't need advice from a teacher."

He sat back then, his legs out in front of him, in that familiar posture of men who feel entirely at home. "Miss Ambrose, you are wise, as well as clean," he teased.

"And you, sir, are dirty," she pointed out. "Mrs. Grey can arrange a bath for you."

She wrapped her blanket around her and started for the door. As she passed his chair, he put out his hand and took hold of hers. "That I will appreciate, Miss A. Do one thing more for me, please."

He did not release her hand, and she felt no inclination to remind him. His touch was warm and dry, and standing there in the parlor, she realized that she was still shivering inside from last night. "And that would be …."

"Reconsider your resolve to leave us on the morning coach, Miss A," he said, and gave her hand a squeeze before he released it. "I need help."

"Indeed you do, my lord," she replied quietly. She left him, spoke to the housekeeper, then returned to the parlor.

She thought he might be asleep, but he remained as she had left him, leaning his chin on his hand, his eyes half closed. He had tried to dab some of the soot from his eyes, because the area under them was smudged. Without comment, she took his handkerchief from him and wiped his face carefully. He watched her the whole time, but for some unaccountable reason, she did not feel shy.

When she finished, she sat down again. "How bad is the damage to the house?"

"Bad enough, I think," he said with a grimace. "When the Rumford was installed, the place where the pipe runs into the chimney must have settled. Ashes have been gathering behind it for some time now, I would imagine. It's not really something a sweep would have noticed." He shook his head. "That portion of the house is three hundred years old, so I can not involve the builder in any litigation."

She smiled at him. "I'm glad you can joke about it, Lord Trevor. It didn't seem so funny last night, standing on the lawn."

"No, it wasn't." His face grew serious. "Miss Ambrose, I'm a little embarrassed to ask you, but I hope I did not leave bruises on your waist."

"You did," she replied, feeling warmth on her own face. "I put it down to your determination to get me down the stairs in a strange house."

He sat back. "This isn't shaping up to be much of a Christmas, is it?"

It seemed a strange remark, one that required a light reply. "No, indeed," she said. "I mean, you were planning to spend it in the City, weren't you, going over legal briefs, or …."

"Depositions, my dear, depositions," he corrected. "And now we have cranky children on our hands, and a broken house."

How quickly he seemed to have included her in the family. "You needn't try to appeal to my better nature," she teased. "I will stay for the duration, bruises or not. Only give me my orders and tell me what you want done here today."

"That is more like it!" he said. He stood up and stretched. "Let Mrs. Grey be your guide. I am certain there is enough cleaning here to keep the children busy. If they complain, remind them that the servants are involved at the hall."

"Very well." Cecilia stood next to him, noting that she came up only to his shoulder. "Perhaps you could take David with you to York, Lord Trevor," she suggested. "He so misses his mother, and he told me that he has already had the measles."

Lord Trevor shook his head. "I dare not, Miss Ambrose. What I did not tell anyone last night was that the letter was from their mother, and not my brother Hugo, who is ill from the measles himself. I am riding to York most specifically to see how he does."

"Oh, my!" Cecilia exclaimed. "Is his life in danger?"

Lord Trevor shrugged. "That is the principal reason I'm leaving here as soon as possible, and without the encumbrance of a little boy, who would only be anxious."

"I promise to keep everyone quite busy here," she assured him.

"Excellent!" He stretched again, and then placed his hand briefly upon her shoulder. "Don't allow any of the children near the manor, either, if you please," he said, his voice quite serious. "I do not trust the timbers in that old place yet, not without an engineer to check it for soundness. The servants will bring over whatever clothing and books are needed." He wrinkled his nose. "And it will all smell of smoke."

He stopped in the doorway, and put his hand to his forehead. "Hell's bells, Miss Ambrose! Do excuse that … I don't see how we can possibly have that annual dinner and dance on Christmas Eve."

"A dinner!" she exclaimed.

"It is the neighborhood's crowning event, which I have managed to avoid for years." He rubbed his eye. "My sister-in-law used to trot out all the local beauties and try to convince them that I was a worthy catch." He shuddered elaborately, to her amusement. "Maybe that is why I have never stayed for Christmas. No, the dinner must be cancelled. I will retrieve the guest list from the manor, and you can assign the imperious Janet the task of written apology to all concerned." He started for the door.

"Or I can go get the list while you bathe."

"No!"

His vehemence startled her. Before she could assure him that she didn't mind a return to the manor, he stood in front of the parlor door, as though to bar her way. "Miss Ambrose, I'd really rather no one from this house went to the manor. The soot is a trial, and the smoke quite clogs the throat."

"Very well, then," she agreed, gratified not a little by his concern. "I'm hardly a shrinking violet, my lord," she murmured.

He smiled at her, and she could have laughed at the effect of very white teeth in a black face. "Well, then, you may get your list, once you have bathed," she said, acutely aware that she had no business telling the second son of a marquis what to do.

"What a nag you are, Miss Ambrose," he told her. He turned toward the hall. "I will wash and then get the list. If that does not meet with your whole approval, let me know now."

She laughed, quite at ease again. "And comb your hair, too! My father used to tell me that if you can't be a good example, you can always be a bad one." Lord, what am I saying? she asked herself.

Lord Trevor seemed to think it completely normal. He nodded to her, and winked. In another moment she heard him whistling on the stairs.

SHE WAS FINISHING HER eggs and toast in the breakfast room when Lord Trevor came into the room. He lofted the guest list at her, and it glided to her plate. He then leaned against the sideboard with the bacon platter in his hand and ate from it.

"You have rag manners," she scolded, "or is this a typical breakfast in the City?"

"No, indeed," he assured her. He finished the bacon, and

looked at the baked eggs, then back at her. She raised her eyebrows and handed him a plate. "Breakfast is usually a sausage roll from a vendor's stall in front of Old Bailey." He put two eggs on his plate and sat beside her. "*This* is Elysian Fields, Miss Ambrose. I should visit my dear brother more often. Not only is the food free, it is well cooked and must be eaten sitting down."

He finished his eggs, then tipped back in his chair and reached for a piece of toast from the sideboard. "Do I dare wipe up this plate with toast?" he asked.

"Would it matter what I said?" she countered, amused. He was the antithesis of everything that Miss Dupree attempted to teach her select females, and quite the last man on earth for any lady of quality. Why that should be a concern for her, she had no clue. The idea came unbidden out of some little closet in her mind. "Do you really care?"

"Nope." He wiped up the plate. "I did ask, though," he said, before finishing the toast. "I probably ought to get a proper cook in my house, and maybe even a butler," he said, as though he spoke more to himself.

She thought he was going to leave then, but he turned slightly in his chair to face her. "Since we have already decided that I have no manners, would you mind my comment, Miss Ambrose, that you really don't look English?"

Her face felt warm again. When the embarrassment passed, she decided that she did not mind his question. "People usually just stare, my lord," she told him. "Politely, of course. My parents went to Egypt to study old documents, and do good. Perhaps you have heard of philanthropists like them. They found me on the steps of Alexandria's oldest archive. They could only assume that whoever left me there had seen them coming and going." She smiled. "They suspect that an erring Englishwoman from Alexandria's foreign community became too involved with an Egyptian of unexalted parentage."

"How diverting to be found, and at a dusty old archive," he

said, without even batting an eye. "Much more interesting than the usual garden patch, or 'tucked up under mama's heart' entrance."

Is there *anything* you won't say? she thought in delight. "It's better. There was a note pinned to my rather expensive blanket, declaring I was a half-English love child."

He threw back his head and laughed. "That certainly trumps being a duty!"

"Yes, certainly," she agreed, trying not to laugh. "My foster mother named me Cecilia because she is a romantic doing *homage* to the patron saint of music." She looked at him, waiting for him to draw back a little or change the subject. To her delight, he did neither.

"Which means, as far as I can tell, that you will always look better in bright colors than nine-tenths of the population, and you probably will never burn in the sun, and should curly hair be in vogue, you are in the vanguard of fashion." He stood up. "Miss Cecilia Ambrose, you are quite the most exotic guest ever to visit this boring old manor. Do whip my nieces and nephew in line, and render a thorough report this evening! Good day to you, kind lady. Thank you for rescuing me from utter boredom this Christmas."

He left the room as quickly as he had entered it. For the tiniest minute, it seemed as though he had sucked all the air out with him. She was still smiling when she heard the front door close behind him. My lord, you are the exotic, she thought, not me. She took a final sip of her tea. I think it is time I woke the sleeping darlings in this lovely little house and put them all to work.

SHE GOT OFF TO a rocky start. Lady Janet had no intention of turning a hand to dust or sweep the floors after the footman removed the elegant carpets to beat out the dust. "Lysander would be aghast," she declared. "I shan't, and you can't compel me."

Lucy gasped at her sister's rudeness. "I *always* do what Miss Ambrose says."

"You're supposed to," her sister sniffed. "You're still in school." She glared at Cecilia. "I have a grievance about this, and I will speak to my uncle when he returns. I will remind him that I Have Come Out."

"From under a rock," David muttered. He looked at Cecilia. "I do not know why my Uncle Trevor did not let me accompany him."

"Nor I," replied Lady Janet with a sniff. "Then we would be rid of a nasty little brother who would try a saint. I am going to write to Lysander this instant! I know my darling will rescue me from this … this …."

"Your home?" Cecilia asked quietly. "Very well. Do write to him. Lucinda and I will dust, and then we will make beds." She noted the triumphant look that Janet gave her younger sister. "Lady Janet, when you have posted your letter to your fiancé, your uncle specifically asked me to have you write to your family's guests and tell them the Christmas dinner is canceled."

"No party?" Janet shrieked, her voice reaching the upper registers.

You could use a week or two at Miss Dupree's, Cecilia thought as she tried not to wince. "Not unless you think there is room for one hundred in the front parlor here, Lady Janet. Just give them the reason why, and offer your parents' apologies," she replied. "Your uncle has also gone to York, not only to see your parents and sister, but to procure workmen enough to put this place to rights again. Apparently there was considerable smoke damage, and the floor downstairs suffered."

Lady Janet's offended silence almost made the air hum. Cecilia touched Davy on the shoulder. "If you could help Lucinda and me, I'm certain we could ask the footman to fetch your uncle's briefs from the manor, and you could continue alphabetizing them."

"I can do that." Davy looked at his older sister, who had

devoted all her attention to the still life over the sideboard. He glared at her rigid back, shrugged, and gestured to his other sister. "C'mon, Lucinda. I'll wager that I can dust the bookroom before you're halfway through the first bedchamber!"

So it went. Lord Trevor returned after dinner, when the fragrance of roasted meat and gravy had settled in the rooms like a benevolent spirit. They had finished eating before he began. Her voice firm, Cecilia told them to wait in the sitting room and allow him to eat in peace before they pounced on him. She held her breath, but Lady Janet only gave her a withering look before flouncing into the sitting room.

When the children were seated, Cecilia excused herself and went to the breakfast room, where Lord Trevor, leaning his hand on his chin, was finishing the last of the rice pudding. He looked up and smiled when she sat down.

"Was it the mutiny on the *Bounty*, Captain Bligh?" he teased.

"Very nearly," she replied. "Lady Janet wrote what I must imagine was an impassioned letter, begging for release, then condescended to write letters of apology to the guests. We tossed bread and water into the room. At least she did not have to gnaw her leg out of a trap to escape."

Lord Trevor laughed. "God help you, Miss Ambrose! Whenever I am tempted to marry and breed, I only have to think of Janet, and temptation recedes. Was Lucinda biddable?"

"Very much so, although she remains ill-used because her sister barely acknowledges her. Davy alphabetized your 1808 cases, and I started him on 1809."

"You are excellent," he said. He drained his teacup and stood up. "Let me brave the sitting room now, and listen to my ill-used, much-abused relatives."

She held out a hand to stop him. "Lord Trevor, how is your brother?"

Lord Trevor frowned. "He is better, but really can't leave before Christmas, no matter how I pleaded and groveled!" He leaned toward her. "He wants you to continue whatever it is you're doing, and not abandon his children to my ramshackle care."

She opened her eyes wider at that artless declaration. "Surely neither he nor Lady Falstoke have any qualms about you."

"They have many," he assured her. He bowed slightly, and indicated that she precede him through the door. "Miss Ambrose, whether you realize it or not, we are an odd pair. You were found on the steps of an archive—still quite romantical, to my way of thinking—and I am the black sheep."

He nudged her forward with a laugh. "When the little darlings in the sitting room have spilled out all their umbrage and ill-usage and flounced off to bed, I will fill you in on my dark career." He took her by the arm in the hall. "But you have already agreed to help me, and I know you would never go back on your word and abandon this household, however sorely you are tried, eh?"

If she had thought to bring along her sketchbook, Cecilia would have had three studies in contrast in the sitting room: Janet looked like a storm was about to break over her head. Lucinda picked at a loose thread in her dress and seemed to swell with questions. Davy, on the other hand, smiled at his uncle.

When Trevor entered the room and sat himself by the fire, they all began at once, Janet springing up to proclaim her ill-usage; Lucinda worried about her parents and whether Christmas would come with them so far removed; and Davy eager to tell his uncle that 1808 was safely filed. Lord Trevor held up his hand. "One moment, my dears," he said, and there was enough edge in his voice to encourage Janet to resume her seat. He looked at his eldest niece. "I am certain that your first concern is for your older sister and her family in York. All are much improved. I knew you wanted to know that." He turned to his nephew, and held out his hand to him. Davy did not hesitate to sit on his lap. Trevor ruffled his hair and kissed his cheek. "That is from your mother! She misses you."

Oh, you do have the touch, Cecilia thought as Davy relaxed against his uncle. "And I hear that you have finished my 1808 cases and started on 1809." Trevor put his arms around his nephew. "Do you think your mama would let me take you back to the City with me and become my secretary?"

"She would miss me," Davy said solemnly. "P'rhaps in a year or two."

"I shall look forward to it." Trevor smiled at Lucinda. "I hear that you have been helping all day to make this little place presentable. My thanks, Lucy."

Lucinda blushed and smiled at Cecilia. "Miss Ambrose says I will someday be able to command an entire household." She looked at her teacher, and her eyes were shy. "A duke's, even."

Janet laughed, but there was no humor in it. "Possibly when pigs fly, Lucinda," she snapped. "Uncle, I …."

"What you should do is apologize to your sister," Trevor said. "Your statement was somewhat graceless."

Lucinda was on her feet then, her face even redder, her eyes filled with tears. "I … I think I will go to bed now, Uncle Trevor. It's been a long day. Davy?" He followed her from the room. With a look at Lord Trevor, Cecilia rose quietly and joined them in the hall. She closed the door behind her, but not quick enough to escape Janet's words.

"I hope you do not expect us to take orders from that foreign woman, Uncle. That is outside of enough, and not to be tolerated. *Who* on earth is *she*?"

Cecilia closed the door as quietly as she could, her face hot. It's not the first insult, she reminded herself, and surely won't be the last. She turned to the children, who looked at her with stricken expressions, and put her finger to her lips. "Let's just go upstairs, my dears," she told them. "I do believe your uncle has his hands full now."

Even through the closed door, they could hear Janet's voice rising. Cecilia hurried up the stairs to escape the sound of it, with the children right behind. At the top of the stairs, Davy took her hand. "Miss Ambrose, I don't feel that way," he told her, his voice as earnest as his expression.

She hugged him. "I know you don't, my dear. Your sister is just upset with this turn of events. I am certain she did not mean what she said."

"You're too kind, Miss Ambrose," Lucinda said.

I'm nothing of the sort, Cecilia thought later after she closed the door to her pupil's room, after helping her into a nightgown, and listening to her prayers for her older sister's family and her parents, marooned in York with the measles.

"No, I am not kind, Lucy dear," she said softly. "I am fearful." She thought she had learned years ago to disregard the sidelong glances and the boorish questions, because to take offense at each one would be a fruitless venture. As much as she loved England now, after a lifetime spent in Egypt, it took little personal persuasion to keep her at Madame Dupree's safe haven. She doubted that she ever went beyond a three-block radius in Bath. I have made myself a prisoner, she thought, and the idea startled her so much that she could only stand there and wonder at her own cowardice.

Reluctant to go downstairs again, she knocked softly on the door of the room that Davy was sharing with his uncle. Better to be in there, she thought, than to have to run into Lady Janet and her spite on the stairs. Davy lay quietly as she had left him, reading in bed, his knees propped up to hold the book. She looked closer, and smiled. He was also fast asleep. She carefully took the book from him, marked the place, and set it on the bedside table. She watched him a moment, enjoying the way his face relaxed in slumber.

I would like to have a boy like you someday, she thought, and the very idea surprised her, because she had never considered it before. I wonder why ever not, she asked herself, then knew the answer before any further reflection. Even though her foster parents had endowed her with a respectable dowry, she had no expectations, not in a country whose people did not particularly relish the exotics among them.

To keep her thoughts at bay, she went around the room quickly, folding Davy's clothes that had been brought over from the manor and placing them in the bureau. He shared the room with his uncle, whose own clothes were jumbled on top of the bureau. Several legal-sized briefs rested precariously on his clothes, along with a pair of spectacles. She wondered if he even had a tailor, and decided that he did not, considering that his public appearances probably found him in a curled peruke and a black robe, which could easily hide a multitude of fashion sins.

She heard light feet on the stairs, and remained where she was until they receded down the short hall to Lucinda's room. The door slammed, and Davy sighed and turned onto his side. She left the room, but it occurred to her that she did not know where to go. She had arranged to sleep on a cot in the little dressing room, but wild horses could not drag her in there now. To go downstairs would mean having to face further embarrassment from Lord Trevor. She knew he would be well meaning, but that would only add to the humiliation. Perhaps I can go below stairs, she thought, then reconsidered. All the servants' rooms in this small dower house were probably full, too, considering that things were a mess at the manor. She also reckoned that a descent below stairs would only confirm Lady Janet's opinion of her.

Cecilia sat on the stairs and leaned against the banister, wishing herself away from the turmoil, uncertain what to do. Probably Lord Trevor would understand now if she wanted to leave in the morning, even if she had promised she would stay. It was safe in Bath. She shook her head, uneasy with the truthfulness of it.

"Is this seat taken?"

She looked up in surprise, shy again, but amused in spite of herself. "No. There are plenty of steps. You need only choose."

Lord Trevor climbed the stairs and sat on the step below her. He yawned, then rested his back against the banister. She didn't want him to say anything, because she didn't want his pity, but she was too timid to begin the conversation. When, after a lengthy silence, he did speak, he surprised her.

"Miss Ambrose, I wish you had slapped my wretched niece silly, instead of just closed the door on her. You have oceans more forbearance than I will ever possess."

"I doubt that, sir," she said, and chose her own words carefully, since he was doing the same. "I've learned that protestation is rarely effective."

"Not the first time, eh?" he asked, his voice casual.

"And probably not the last." She rose to go—where she did not know—but Lord Trevor took her hand and kept her where she was. "I ... I do hope you were not too harsh with her."

He released his hold on her. "Just stay put a while, Miss Ambrose, if you will," he told her. "I was all ready to haul her over my knee and give her a smack." He chuckled. "That probably would have earned me a chapter in the tome she is undoubtedly going to write to her precious Lysander in the morning."

"But you didn't."

"No, indeed. I merely employed that tactic I learned years ago from watching some of the other barristers who plead in court, and looked her up and down until her knees knocked. Then I told her I was ashamed of her." He leaned his elbow on the tread above and looked at her. "And I am, Miss Ambrose. Believe me, I am."

The look that he gave her was so contrite that she felt tears behind her eyelids. I had better make light of this, she thought. I'm sure he wants me to assure him that it is all right, and that I didn't mind. She forced herself to look him in the eye. Even in the gloom of the stairwell, she could tell that nothing of the sort was on his mind. She had never seen a more honest gaze.

"I won't deny that it hurt, Lord Trevor," she replied, her voice quiet, "but do you know, I've been sitting here and thinking that it's been pretty easy the last few holidays to hide myself in Bath. And ... and I really have nothing to hide, do I?"

There. She had told a near stranger something that she could not even write to her mother, when that dear woman had written many times from India to ask her how she really did, on her own and without the protection of her distinguished missionary family.

Again he surprised her. He took her hand and held it. "Nothing to hide at all, my dear Miss Ambrose. Would it surprise you that I have been doing that very thing? I have been confining myself to the area of my rooms near Lincoln's Inn and Old Bailey for nearly eleven years. We are more alike than my silly niece would credit."

Her bewilderment must have shown on her face, because he stood up and pulled her up, too. "If you're not too tired, or too irritated at the ignorance and ill-will in one little dower house, I believe I want to explain myself. My dear, do you care for sherry?"

"If it's good sherry."

"The best that smugglers can find! I'd forgotten how excellent my brother's wine cellar is. Do join me in the sitting room. Miss Ambrose."

She didn't really have a choice, because he never released her hand. Mystified rather than embarrassed now, she followed him into the sitting room. He let go of her hand to pull another chair close to the fireplace, and indicated that she sit. She did, with a sigh. The fire was just warm enough, and the pillow he had placed behind her back just the right touch. He poured her a glass of sherry from the table between them, handed it to her, then sat in the other chair and propped his feet on the fender.

"I told you I am the black sheep, didn't I?"

She had to laugh. "And I am, well, a little colorful, too." He joined in her laughter, not the least self-conscious, which warmed her heart. He surprised her by quickly leaning forward to touch her cheek. "Your skin is the most amazing shade of olive. Ah, is that the Egyptian in you? How fine! And brown eyes that are probably the envy of nations." He chuckled. "I don't mean to sound like a rakehell, Miss A." He looked at the far wall. "I suppose I am used to speaking my mind."

"I suppose that's your privilege," she said.

He took a sip of sherry. "I do say what I please. I doubt anyone in the *ton* thinks I am a gentleman."

"You're the brother of a marquis," she reminded him. "Surely that counts for …."

"It counts for nothing," he interrupted, finishing her thought. "I am not playing the game I was born to play, Miss Ambrose, and some take offense."

She sat up straight and turned to face him impulsively. "How can you say that? I have been reading of the good you have done!"

"You are too kind, my dear." He poured another drink. "When I was in York today, I spoke to the warden at the Abbey. You're from a crusading family, yourself, aren't you?"

She nodded. "Papa and Mama lived in Egypt for nearly twenty years. I am not their only 'extra child,' as Papa puts it."

"The warden was sufficiently impressed when I mentioned that a member of the Ambrose family was visiting the Marquis of Falstoke."

Cecilia smiled and swirled the sherry in her glass. "And now they are doing good in India, and plumbing the depths of Sanskrit." She looked up, pleased to see Lord Trevor smiling at her, for no particular reason that she could discern. At least he does not look so tired, she thought. "We came to England in 1798, when I was sixteen. I went four years to Miss Dupree's Select Academy, and now I teach drawing and pianoforte."

"You weren't tempted to go to India with them?"

"No, I was not," she said. He was still smiling at her, and she decided he was a most attractive man, even with his untidy hair and rumpled clothing. "I like it right here, even with …

with its occasional difficulties." She set down the wineglass. "And that is all I am going to say now. It is your turn to tell me why someone of your rank and quality thinks he is a black sheep."

"It's a sordid tale," he warned her.

"I doubt that. Slide the hassock over, please. Thank you."

He made himself comfortable, too. "Miss Ambrose, the fun of being a younger son cannot be underrated. I did a double first at Oxford, contemplated taking Holy Orders, considered buying a pair of colors, and even thought I would travel to the Caribbean and invest in sugar cane and slaves."

She relaxed, completely at ease. "That sounds sufficiently energetic."

"I didn't have to *do* anything. Some younger sons must scramble about, I suppose, but our father was a wealthy man, and our mother equally endowed. She willed me her fortune. I am better provided for than most small countries."

"My congratulations," she murmured. "You know, so far this is not sordid. I have confiscated more daring stories from my students late at night, when they were supposed to be studying."

"Let me begin the dread tale of my downfall from polite society before you fall asleep and start to snore," he told her.

"You're the one who snores, according to Davy," she reminded him.

"And you must be a sore trial to the decorum of Miss Deprave's Select Academy," he teased.

"*Dupree*," she said, trying not to laugh.

"If you insist," he teased, then settled back. "I suppose I was running the usual course for second sons, engaging in one silly spree after another. It changed one evening at White's, while I was listening to my friends argue heatedly for an hour about whether to wear white or red roses in their lapels. It was an epiphany, Miss Ambrose."

"I don't suppose there are too many epiphanies in White's," she said.

"That may have been the first! I decided the very next morning, after my head cleared, to toddle over to Lincoln's Inn and see about the law. My friends were aghast, and concerned for my sanity, but do you know, Miss A, it suited me right down to the ground. I sat for law through several years, ate my required number of dinners at the Inn, and was called to the Bar."

"My congratulations. I would say that makes you stodgy rather than sordid."

He smiled at her, real appreciation in his eyes. "Miss Ambrose, you are a witty lady with a sharp tongue! Should I pity poor Janet if she actually tries your kindness beyond belief and you give her what she deserves?"

She was serious then. "She is young, and doesn't know what she says."

"Spoken like the daughter of the well churched!" He leaned across the table and touched her arm. "Here comes the sordid part. Miss A." And then his face was more serious than hers. "I went to Old Bailey one cold morning to shift some toff's heir from a cell where he'd languished—the three D's, m'dear: drunk, disorderly, and disturbing the peace. It was a matter of fifteen minutes, a plea to the magistrate, and a whopping fine for Papa to pay. Just fifteen minutes." He stood up, went to the fireplace, and stared into the flames. "There was a little boy in the docket ahead of my client. I could have bumped him and gone ahead. I had done it before, and no magistrate ever objected."

Cecilia slid her glass aside and tucked her legs under her. Have you ever told anyone this before? she wanted to ask. Something in his tone suggested that he had not, and she wondered why he was speaking to her. Of course, Mrs. Dupree always did say that people liked to confide in her. "It's your special gift, dearie," her employer had told her on more than one occasion.

"There he stood, not more than seven years old, I think, with only rags to cover him, and it was a frosty morning. It was all he could do to hold himself upright, so frightened was he."

She must have made some sound, because Lord Trevor looked at her. He sat down on the hassock. "Did he … was he represented?" she asked.

He nodded, his face a study in contempt. "They all are. We call ourselves a law-abiding nation, Miss A, don't we? His rep was one of the second year boys at Gray's Inn, getting a practice in. Getting a practice in! My God!"

Impulsively she leaned forward and touched his arm. He took her hand and held it. Something in her heart told her not to pull away. "He had copped two loaves of bread and, of all things, a pomegranate." Lord Trevor passed his free hand in front of his eyes. "The magistrate boomed at him, 'Why the pomegranate, you miscreant?' " He put her hand to his cheek. "The boy said, 'Because it's Christmas, your worship.' "

Cecilia felt the tears start in her eyes. She patted his cheek, and he released her hand, an apologetic look in his eyes. "Miss A, you'll think I'm the most forward rake who ever walked the planet. I don't know what I was thinking."

"*I* am thinking that you need to talk to people now and then," she told him.

He tried to smile, and failed. "His sentence was transportation to Van Diemen's Land. Some call it Tasmania. It is an entire island devoted to criminals, south of Australia. Poor little tyke fainted on the spot, and everyone in the courtroom laughed, my client loudest of all."

"You didn't laugh."

"No. All I saw was a little boy soiling his pants from fear, with not an advocate in the world, not a mother or father in sight, sentenced to a living death." He looked at her, and she saw the tears on his face. "And this is English justice," he concluded quietly.

She could think of nothing to say, beyond the fact that she knew it was better to be silent than to let some inanity tumble out of her face, after his narrative. She glanced at him, and his own gaze was unwavering upon her. She realized he was seeking permission from her to continue. "There must be more," she said finally. "Tell me."

He seemed to relax a little with the knowledge that she was not too repulsed to hear the rest. "Is it warm in here?" he asked, running his finger around his frayed collar.

"Yes, and isn't that delightful? I never can get really *warm* in this country!" she countered. "Don't stall me, sir. You have my entire attention."

He continued. "I could not get that child out of my mind. In the afternoon I went back to Old Bailey, found the magistrate— he was so bored—and went to Newgate."

Cecilia shivered. Lord Trevor nodded. "You're right to feel a little frisson, Miss A. It's a terrible place." He grimaced. "I know it must be obvious to you that I am no Brummel. Nowadays, when I know I'm going to Newgate, I wear my Newgate clothes. I keep them in a room off the scullery at my house because I cannot get the smell out." He sighed. "Well, that was blunt, eh? I found Jimmy Daw—that was his name—in a cell with a score of older criminals. I gave him an old coat of mine."

Lord Trevor hung his head down. Cecilia had an almost overwhelming urge to touch his hair. She kept her hands clenched in her lap.

"My God, Miss A, he thanked me and wished me a happy Christmas!"

"Oh, dear," she breathed. She got up then and walked to the window and back again, because she knew she did not wish to hear the rest of his story. He stood, too, his lips tight together. He went to the fireplace again and rested his arm on the mantel.

"You know where this is going, don't you?" he asked, surprised.

She nodded. "I have lived a little in the world, my lord. I'm also no child."

"The magistrate met me in my chambers the next morning—

it was Christmas Day—to tell me that those murderers, cutpurses, and thieves had tortured and killed Jimmy for the coat that I left for him, in my naïveté."

She could tell by looking at his eyes that the event might have happened yesterday. "That is hard, indeed, sir," she murmured, and sat down again, mainly because her legs would not hold her. She took a deep breath, and another, until her head did not feel so detached. "I did not know about Jimmy," she said softly, "but I told you that I have read about your work—or some of it—in the papers. I know you have made amends."

"With a vengeance, Miss A, with a vengeance," he assured her. "That frivolous fop I bailed out the day before had the distinction of being my last client among the titled and wealthy. I am a children's advocate now. When they come in the docket, I represent as many as I can. Yes, some are transported—I cannot stop the workings of justice—but they are *not* incarcerated with men old enough to do them evil, and they go to Australia, instead of Van Diemen's Land. It is but a small improvement, but the best I can do."

"How did ... how did you manage that?"

He smiled for the first time in a long while. "Like all good barristers, I know the value of blackmail, Miss A! Let us just say that I lawyered away a juicy bit of scandal for our dear Prinny, and he owed me massively. God knows he has no interest in anyone's welfare but his own, but even he has a small bit of influence."

It was her turn to relax a little, relieved that his tone was lighter. She could not imagine the conditions under which he labored, and she had the oddest wish to hold him close and comfort him as a mother would a child. "Lord Trevor, I think what you are doing is noble. Why do you say that you are the family's black sheep?"

He sat down again and took another sip of his sherry, then looked at her over the rim of the glass. "It is your turn to be naïve. What I do, and where and how I do it, has cut me off completely from my peers. It is as though I wear my Newgate clothes everywhere. No one extends invitations to me, and I am the answer to no maiden's prayer."

"And people of your class are a little embarrassed to be seen with you, and you don't really have a niche," she said, understanding him perfectly, because she understood herself. "That life has made you bold and outspoken, and it has made me shy."

She looked at him with perfect understanding, and he smiled back. "We are both black sheep, Miss Ambrose," he said.

"How odd." Another thought occurred to her. "Why are you here?"

To answer her, he reached in his vest pocket and pulled out a folded sheet. "You may not be aware that my niece Lucinda has been writing to me."

"She did mention you in sketching class once," Cecilia said, and her comprehension grew. She put her hand to her mouth. "Oh! She said you worked with children, and several of the other pupils started to laugh! Their parents must have …."

"I told you I am a hiss and a byword in some circles. I sometimes keep stray children at my house until I can find situations for them." He hesitated.

"Go on," she told him. "I doubt there is anything you can say now that would surprise me."

"There might be," he replied. "Well! Some of my peers think I am a sodomite. These things are whispered about. Who knows what parents tell their children."

"Really, Lord Trevor," she said. "It *is* warm in here."

He crossed the room, and threw up the window sash. "I assure you I do *not* practice buggery, Miss A! What I do have are enlightened friends who are willing to take these children to agricultural settings and employ them gainfully."

"Bravo, sir," she said softly.

"I do it for Jimmy Daw." He tapped the letter. "Lucinda tells me how unhappy she is, and damn it, I've been neglecting my own family."

"She is sad and uncomfortable to see her sister growing away from her," Cecilia agreed. "I had wanted to talk to Lady Falstoke about that very thing. I suppose that is why I came."

He folded the letter and put it back in his waistcoat. "I came here with the intention of giving them a prosy lecture about gratitude, well larded with examples of children who have so much less than they do." He rubbed his hands together. "Thank God for a fire in the chimney! Now we are thrown together in close quarters to get reacquainted. Do you think there is silver to polish below stairs?"

She laughed. "If there is not, you will find it!" She grew serious again. "There is more to this than a prosy lecture, isn't there? Lord Trevor, when did Jimmy Daw ...."

"Eleven years ago on Christmas Eve," he answered. "Miss Ambrose, for all that time I have thrown myself into my work, and ignored my own relations." He shook his head. "I see them so seldom."

She went to the window and closed it, now that the room was cooler, or at least she was not feeling so embarrassed by this singular man's blunt plain speaking. "I must own to a little sympathy for them, Lord Trevor. Here they are, stuck in close quarters with two people that they don't know well. It is nearly Christmas, and their parents are away."

He winked at her. "Should we go easy on the little blokes?"

"Lord Trevor, *where* do you get your language?" she said in exasperation.

"From the streets, ma'am," he told her, not a bit ruffled. "I feel as though I have been living on them for the past eleven years."

"That may be something that must change, sir," she replied.

He laughed and opened the window again. "Too warm for me, Miss Ambrose! You are an educator *and* a manager? Did one of your ancestors use a lash on those poor Israelites in Egypt?"

"Stuff and nonsense!" She went to the door. "And now I am going to bed." She stopped, and she frowned. "Except that...." Be a little braver, she ordered herself, if you think to be fit company this week for a man ten times braver than you. "I have no intention of sleeping on that servant's cot in the girls' chamber, not after the snippy way Lady Janet treated me! She already thinks of me as a servant, and I have no intention of encouraging that tendency. Is the sofa in the book room comfortable, sir?"

"I don't know. Seems as though we ought to do better for you than a couch in the office, Miss A," he told her as he joined her at the door.

"Are all dower houses this small?"

"I rather doubt it. Some of my ancestors must have been vastly frugal! What say you brave the sofa tonight, and we'll see if we can find you a closet under the stairs, or a secret room behind some paneling off the kitchen where the Chase family used to hide Royalists."

He tagged along while she went downstairs to the linen closet and selected a sheet and blanket. He found a pillow on a shelf. "You could sleep in here," he told her. "You're small enough to crawl onto that lower shelf."

She laughed out loud, then held out her hand to him. "I am going upstairs now. What plans do you have, if Sir Lysander whisks Janet away from this?"

He was still holding her hand. He released it, and handed her the pillow. "I happen to know Lysander's parents." They left the linen closet. "He is an only child, and my stars, Miss A, they are careful with him." He looked toward the ceiling. "Do you happen to know if she mentioned measles in her letter?"

"You can be certain I was not allowed to look at the letter." They started for the stairs. "Besides, the contagion is in York, and not here."

He only smiled. "Did I mention they are careful parents? Good night, m'dear."

THE SOFA IN THE book room realized her worst fears, but Cecilia was so tired that she slept anyway. When she finally woke, it was to a bright morning. She sat up, stretched, then went to the window. Lord Trevor had spent his time well in York, she decided. A veritable army of house menders had turned into the family property and were heading in carts toward the manor.

Someone knocked. She put her robe on over her nightgown and opened the door upon Lord Trevor. "Good morning, sir," she told him.

"It is, isn't it?" He grinned at her. "Miss A, what a picture you are!"

Her hands went to her hair. "I can never do anything with it in the morning. You are a beast to mention it."

He stepped back as if she had stabbed him. "Miss A! I was going to tell you how much I like short, curly hair! No lady wears it these days, and more's the pity." He winked at her. "Is it hard to drag a comb through such a superabundance of curls?"

"A perfect purgatory," she assured him. "I used a comb with very wide teeth." She felt her face go red. Mrs. Dupree would be shocked at this conversation. "Enough about my toilette, sir! What are your plans?"

"I am off to the manor to get the renovation started. Mrs. Grey will accompany me. She has set breakfast, and left one servant, should you need to send a message."

"And did she locate a plethora of silver begging for polish?"

"Indeed she did! There is more than enough to keep my relatives in cozy proximity with each other."

"If they choose to be so," she reminded him. "Sir Lysander …."

He put a finger to her lips. "Miss A, trust me there." He took his hand away, and she watched in unholy glee as his face reddened. "Sorry! And Janet is to apologize."

"Only if she means it," Cecilia said softly.

"She will," he told her, then leaned closer. "I am not her favorite uncle, at the moment, however." He straightened up. "I'll be back as soon as I can. Do carry on."

He left, and she suffered another moment of indecision before straightening her back and mounting the stairs to the room where the girls slept. They were awake and sitting up when she came in the room and pulled back the draperies. She took a deep breath, not wanting to look at Lady Janet and see the scorn in her eyes.

"Good morning, ladies," she said, her voice quiet but firm. "Your uncle has gone to the manor to direct the work there, and breakfast is ready." She took another deep breath. "Lady Janet, there are letters to finish. Lady Lucinda, you and your brother may wish to begin polishing some silver below stairs. Excuse me please while I dress."

It took all the dignity she could muster to retreat to the dressing room, throw on her clothes, and then pull that comb through her recalcitrant curls. When she came into the chamber again, Lucinda and Janet were making the bed. She almost smiled. The pupils at Mrs. Dupree's all did their own tidying, but Janet was obviously not acquainted with such hard service. Her eyes downcast, her lips tight together, she thumped her pillow down and yanked up the coverlet on her side of the bed. Lucy took a look at her sister and scurried into the dressing room. Cecilia stood by the door, not ready to face Janet, either. Her hand was on the knob when the young lady spoke.

"I am sorry, Miss Ambrose."

She turned around, wishing that her stomach did not churn at the words that sounded as if they were pulled from Janet's throat with tongs. "I know your uncle Trevor meant well, Lady Janet, but I know I am a stranger to you, and perhaps someone you are not accustomed to seeing."

"That doesn't mean I should be rude," Janet said, her voice

quiet. "It seems like there is so much to think of right now, so many plans to make ...." She looked up then, and her expression was shy, almost tentative. "Lucy tells me you are a wonderful artist."

"She is the one with great talent," Cecilia replied, happy to turn the compliment. She returned Janet's glance. "I hope Lord Trevor was not too hard on you."

Janet turned to the bed and smoothed out a nonexistent wrinkle. She shook her head. "I know I will feel better when Lysander arrives."

Well, that is hopeful, Cecilia thought as she went to the next room, woke Davy, then went to the breakfast room. By the time the children came into the room, chose their food, and sat down, her equilibrium had righted itself. Janet said nothing, but Lucinda, after several glances at her sister, began a conversation.

It was interrupted by the housekeeper, who brought a letter on a silver platter. Janet's eyes lighted up. She took it, cast a triumphant glance at the other diners, excused herself, and left the room, her head up.

"I hope Sir Lysander swoops down and carries her away," Davy said.

"Do you not call him just Lysander?" Cecilia asked, curious. "He is going to be your brother in February, is he not?"

Davy rolled his eyes, and Lucinda giggled. "Miss Ambrose, we have been informed that he is *Sir* Lysander to us," Lucinda said. She sighed then. "I hope she stays, Davy."

"Then you are probably the only one at the table with that wish!" her brother retorted. He blushed, and looked at his plate. "I don't mean to embarrass you, Miss Ambrose."

"You don't," she said, and touched his arm. "In fact, I think—"

What she thought left her head before the words were out. A loud scream came from the sitting room, and then noisy tears bordering on the hysterical. Lucinda's eyes opened wide, and

Davy lay back in his chair and lolled his head, as though all hope was gone.

"Oh, dear," Cecilia whispered. "I fear that Sir Lysander did not meet Lady Janet's expectations. She's your sister, and you know her well. Should we *do* anything?"

"I could prop a chair under the door, so she can't get in here," Davy suggested helpfully.

"David, you know that is *not* what Miss Ambrose means!" Lucinda scolded. She looked at Cecilia. "Usually we make ourselves scarce when Janet is in full feather." She stood up. "Davy, I have a craving to go tramping over to the south orchard. There is holly there, and greenery that would look good on the mantelpiece. Would you like to join us, Miss Ambrose?" She had to raise her voice to compete with the storm of tears from the sitting room across the hall, which was now accompanied by what sounded like someone drumming her feet on the floor.

"I think not," Cecilia said. She finished her now-cold tea. "Bundle up warm, children, and take the footman along. You might ask him to stop at the manor and inform your uncle."

Lucinda nodded. She opened the breakfast room door and peeked into the hall. "We don't really want to leave you here alone, Miss Ambrose."

"It is only just a temper tantrum, my dear," Cecilia said, using her most firm educator's voice. "I can manage." I think I can manage, she told herself as the children gave her doubtful glances, then scurried up the stairs to get their coats and mittens. She sat at the table until they left the dower house with the footman. The last person Janet wants to see is me, especially when we have just begun to be on speaking terms, she thought.

"Miss?"

Cecilia looked up to see the housekeeper in the doorway, holding a tray.

"Please come in, Mrs. Grey," she said, managing a half smile.

"We seem to be in a storm of truly awesome dimensions."

Mrs. Grey frowned at the sitting-room door, then came to the table, where she set down the tray. "Between you and me, Miss Ambrose, I think that Sir Lysander is in for the surprise of his life, the first time she does *that* across the breakfast table!"

"Oh, my," Cecilia said faintly. "That will be a cold bath over baked eggs and bacon, will it not!"

Mrs. Grey smiled at her, in perfect agreement. "I am suggesting that you not go in there until she is a little quieter." She indicated the tray. "Lady Falstoke sometimes waves burnt feathers under her nose, and then puts cucumbers on her eyes to cut the swelling." She frowned. "What she really needs is a spoonful of cod-liver oil, and the admonition to act her age but ..." She hesitated.

"...but Lady Falstoke is an indulgent mother," Cecilia continued. "I will give her a few minutes more, then go in there, Mrs. Grey, and be the perfect listener."

The look the housekeeper gave her was as doubtful as the one that Davy and Lucinda left the room with. "I could summon her uncle, except ..."

"...this is a woman's work," Cecilia said. "Perhaps a little sympathy is in order."

"Can you do that? She has been less than polite to you." Mrs. Grey's face was beet red.

"She just doesn't know me," she said, and felt only the slightest twinge of conscience, considering how quick she had been ready to bolt from the place as recently as last night.

Her quietly spoken words seemed to satisfy Mrs. Grey, who nodded and left the room, but not without a backward glance of concern and sympathy as eloquent as speech. She considered Lord Trevor's words of last night, and the kind way he looked at her. If he can manage eleven years of what must be the worst work in the world, she could surely coddle one spoiled niece into a better humor.

She waited until the raging tears had degenerated into sobs

and hiccups, and then silence, before she entered the sitting room. Janet had thrown herself facedown on the sofa. A broken vase against the wall, with succession-house flowers crumbled and twisted around it, offered further testimony of the girl's rage. Janet is one of those people who needs an audience, Cecilia thought. Well, here I am. She set the tray on a small table just out of Janet's reach, and sat down, holding herself very still.

After several minutes, Janet opened her swollen eyes and regarded Cecilia with real suspicion. Cecilia gritted her teeth and smiled back, hoping for a good mix of sympathy and comfort.

"I want my mother," Janet said finally. She sat up and blew her nose vigorously on a handkerchief already waterlogged. "I want her now!"

"I'm certain you do," Cecilia replied. "A young lady needs her mother at a time like this." She held her breath, hoping it was the right thing to say.

"But she is not here!" Janet burst out, and began to sob again. "Was there ever a more wretched person than I!"

I think an hour of horror stories in your uncle's company might suggest to you that perhaps one or two people have suffered just a smidgeon, Cecilia thought. She sat still a moment longer, and then her heart spoke to her head. She got up from her chair, and sat down next to Janet, not knowing what she would do, but calm in the knowledge that the girl was in real agony. After another hesitation, she touched Janet's arm. "I know I am only a poor substitute, but I will listen to you, my lady," she said.

Janet turned her head slowly. The suspicion in her eyes began to fade. Suddenly she looked very young, and quite disappointed. She put a trembling hand to her mouth. "Oh, Miss Ambrose, he doesn't love me anymore!" she whispered.

With a sigh more of relief than empathy, Cecilia put her arm around the girl. "My, but this is a dilemma!" she exclaimed.

She gestured toward the letter crumpled in Janet's hand. "He said *that* in your letter?"

"He might as well have said it!" Janet said with a sob. She smoothed open the message and handed it to Cecilia. "Read it!"

Cecilia took the letter and read of Sir Lysander's regrets, and his fear of contracting any dread diseases.

Janet had been looking at the letter, too. "Miss Ambrose, I wrote most specifically that the measles were confined to my sister's house in York. He seems to think that he will come here and … and die!"

She could not argue with Janet's conclusion. The letter was a recitation of its writer's fear of contagion, putrid sore throat, consumption, and other maladies both foreign and domestic. "Look here," she said, pointing. "He writes here that he will fly to your side, the moment all danger is past."

"He should fly here now! At once!"

Lord Trevor Chase would, Cecilia thought suddenly. If the woman he loved was ill, or in distress, he would leap up from the breakfast table and fork the nearest horse in his rush to be by her side. Nothing would stop him. She sat back, as amazed at her thoughts as she was certain of them. But he was a rare man, she decided. This knowledge that had come to her unbidden warmed her. She tightened her grip on Janet. "My dear, didn't your uncle tell me that Sir Lysander is an only child?"

Janet nodded. She stared sorrowfully at the letter.

"I think we can safely conclude that his parents are overly concerned, and that is the source of this letter." She scanned the letter quickly, hoping that the timid Sir Lysander would not fail her. She sighed with relief; he did not. "And see here, my dear, how he has signed the letter!"

"'You have my devoted, eternal love,'" Janet read. She sniffed. "But not including measles, Miss Ambrose."

"No, not including measles," she echoed. "Surely we can allow him one small fault, Lady Janet, don't you think?" Lady

Janet thought. "Well, perhaps." She raised her handkerchief, and looked at it with faint disgust.

Cecilia pulled her own handkerchief out of her sleeve. "Here, my dear. This one is quite dry."

Janet took it gratefully and blew her nose. "You don't ever cry, Miss Ambrose?"

It was the smallest of jokes, but Cecilia felt the weight of the world melting from her own shoulders. "I wouldn't dare, Lady Janet!" she declared with a laugh. "Only think how that would ruin my credit at Mrs. Dupree's Select Academy." She touched Janet's shoulder. "This can be our secret." She stood up. "I recommend that you recline here again. Mrs. Grey has brought over a cucumber from the succession house. A couple of these slices on your eyes will quite remove all the swelling."

Janet did as she said. Cecilia tucked a light throw around her, then applied the cucumbers. "I would give the cucumber about fifteen minutes. Perhaps then you might finish the rest of those letters."

"I will do that," Janet agreed. The cucumber slices covered her eyes, but she pointed to the letter. "Do you think I should reply to Lysander's sorry letter, Miss Ambrose? I could tell him what I think and make him squirm."

"You could, I suppose, but wouldn't it be more noble of you to assure him that you understand, and look forward to seeing him in a week or so?" Janet's mulish expression, obvious even with the cucumbers, suggested to Cecilia that the milk of human kindness wasn't precisely flowing through Janet's veins yet. "I think it is what your dear mother would do," Cecilia continued, appealing to that higher power.

"I suppose you are right," Janet said reluctantly, after lengthy consideration. "But I will write him *only* after I have finished all the other letters!"

"That will show him!" Cecilia said, grateful that the cucumbers hid her smile from Janet's eyes. "My dear, Christmas can be such a trying time for some people."

"I should say. I do not know when I have suffered more."

Cecilia regarded Janet, who had settled herself quite comfortably into the sofa, cucumber slices and all. My credit seems to be on the rise, she thought. I wonder …. "Lady Janet, perhaps you could help me with something that perplexes me."

The young lady raised one cucumber. "Perhaps. By the time I finish writing lists for wedding plans, I am usually quite fatigued at close of day."

No wonder Lord Trevor remains put off by the topic of reproduction, Cecilia thought. Even on this side of her better nature, Lady Janet is enough to make anyone think twice about producing children. "It is a small thing, truly it is," she said. "Your younger sister seems to have taken the nonsensical notion into her head that you are too busy with wedding plans to even remember that you are sisters."

"Impossible!" Janet declared.

"I agree, Lady Janet, but she is at that trying age of twelve, and feels that you haven't time for her."

"Of course I … well, there may be some truth to that," Janet said. "H'mm."

She was silent then, and it occurred to Cecilia that this was probably more introspection than Janet had ever waded in before. "Something to think about, Lady Janet," she said.

She was in the book room, folding her blanket and wondering where to stash it, when Lady Janet came in. She smiled to see that the cucumbers had done their duty. "Ready to tackle the letters again, my lady?" she asked.

Janet shook her head, then looked at Cecilia shyly. "Not now. I think I will go find Lucinda and David. Did they mention where they were headed?"

"Your sister said something about the south orchard."

"Oh, yes! There is wonderful holly near the fence." She left the room as quickly as she had come into it.

"Someone needs to do these letters," Cecilia told herself when the house was quiet. She sat down at the desk and looked at the last one Janet had written. She picked up the pen to continue, then set it down, with no more desire to do the job than Lady Janet, evidently. She decided to go below stairs, and see if Lord Trevor had carried out his threat to find silver to polish.

She laughed out loud when she entered the servants' dining room to see Lord Trevor, an apron around his waist, sleeves rolled up, rubbing polish on an epergne that was breathtaking in its ugliness. He looked up and grinned at her. "Did ye ever see such a monstrosity?" He looked around her. "And where are my nieces and nephew? Isn't this supposed to be the time I have ordained for my prosy talk on gratitude and sibling affection?" He put down the cloth, and leaned across the table toward her. "Or is this the time when you scold me roundly for abandoning you to the lions upstairs?"

"I should," she told him as she found an apron on a hook and put it around her middle. "Now don't bamboozle me. Did you leave me to face Lady Janet alone when that letter came from her dearly beloved?"

"I cannot lie," he began.

"Of course you can," she said, interrupting him. "You are a barrister, after all."

He slapped his forehead. "I suppose I deserved that."

"You did," she agreed, picking up a cloth. "For a man who fearlessly stalks the halls of Old Bailey, defending London's most vulnerable, you're remarkably cowardly."

"Guilty as charged, mum," he replied cheerfully. "I could never have soothed those ruffled feathers, but it appears that you did." He turned serious then. "And did my graceless niece apologize, too?"

"She is not so graceless, sir!" Cecilia chided. "Some people are more tried and sorely vexed by holidays and coming events than others. We did conclude that Sir Lysander is still the best of men, even though he dares not brave epidemics. We have also resolved to make some amends to Lucinda." She dipped the knife she had been polishing into the water bath. "I, sir, have freed you from the necessity of a prosy lecture! May I return to Bath?"

"No. You promised to stay," he reminded her, and handed her a spoon.

"I'm not needed now," she pointed out, even as she began to polish it. "Hopefully, Lord and Lady Falstoke will be here at Christmas, which will make the dower house decidedly crowded, unless the repairs at the manor can be finished by then. You will have ample time to get to know your nieces and nephew better, and do you know, I think they might not be as ungrateful as you seem to think."

He nodded, and concentrated on the epergne again. She watched his face, and wondered why he seemed to become more serious. Isn't family good cheer what you want? she asked herself.

It was a question she asked herself all that afternoon as she watched him grow quieter and more withdrawn. When the children came back—snow-covered, shivering, but cheerful—from gathering greenery, she watched uneasily how he had to force himself to smile at them. All through dinner, while Davy outlined his plans for the holly, and his sister planned an expedition to the kitchen in the morning to make Christmas sweets, he sat silent, staring at nothing in particular.

He is a man of action, she decided, and unaccustomed to the slower pace of events in country living. He must chafe to return to London. She stared down at her own dinner as though it writhed, then gave herself a mental shake. That couldn't be it. Hadn't he told her earlier that both King's Bench and Common Pleas were not in session? He had also declared that was true of Magistrate's Court, where most of his clients ended. Why could he not relax and enjoy the season, especially since he had come so far, and met with pleasant results so easily? Even after she told him before dinner that Janet had seemed genuinely contrite and willing to listen, he hadn't received the news with any enthusiasm. It was as though he was gearing himself up for a larger struggle. She wished she knew what it was.

Once the children were in bed, she wanted to ask him, but she knew she would never work up the nerve. Instead, she went into the sitting room to read. He joined her eventually, carrying a letter. He sat down and read through the closely written page again. "Maria writes to say that my brother is much better now, and will be home on Christmas Day," he told her.

"And your niece Amelia's brood?"

"Maria says they are all scratching and complaining, which certainly trumps the fever and vacant stare," he told her. He sat back in the chair and stared into the flames.

Now or never, she thought. "Lord Trevor, is there something the matter?"

He looked up quickly from his contemplation of the flames. "No, of course not." He smiled, but the smile didn't even approach his eyes. "Thanks to your help, I think my nieces and nephew will be charting a more even course."

Chilled by the bleakness on his face, she tried to make light of the moment: anything to see the same animation in his face that had been there when she arrived only a few days ago, or even just that morning. "We can really thank Sir Lysander and his fastidious parents."

"Oh? What? Oh, yes, I'm certain you are right," he said. She might as well not have been in the room at all. His mind was miles away, oceans distant. "Well, I think it is time for me to go strangle four or five chickens," she said softly. "And then I will rob the mail coach in my shimmy."

"Ah, yes," he said, all affability. "Good night, Miss Ambrose."

She was a long time getting to sleep that night.

The next day, Christmas Eve, was the same. She woke, feeling decidedly unrested, and sat up on her cot in the dressing room, where the girls had cajoled her to return. Certainly it was better than the book room, and the reasons for avoiding the dressing room seemed to have vanished. Quietly she went into the girls' chamber and looked out the window. Although it was nearly eight o'clock, the sky was only beginning to lighten. The workers from York, who were saying at an inn in the village, were starting to arrive, their wagons and gigs lit with lanterns.

I wonder how much work is left to do there, she thought. If the marquis and marchioness are to return tomorrow, then they must be in a pelter to finish. She stood at the window until her bare feet were cold, then turned toward the dressing room. She moved as quietly as she could, but Janet sat up. "Good morning, Miss Ambrose," she said as she yawned. "Do you want to help Lucinda and me in the kitchen? Mrs. Grey has said we may make however many Christmas treats we want. Think what a welcome that will be for my parents."

Cecilia sat down on the bed beside her, and Janet obligingly shifted her legs. "You'll be glad to see them, won't you, my dear?" Cecilia asked.

"Oh, yes!" Janet touched her arm. "I can only wish they had been here for all of the season, but Amelia needed them." She sighed. "This is my last Christmas at Chase Hall, you know."

Cecilia smiled. "You'll be returning with a husband this time next year."

Janet drew up her legs and rested her chin on her knees. When Lucinda moved, she smoothed the coverlet over her sister's back. "Oh, I know that," she whispered, "but it is never the same, is it?"

"No, it is not," Cecilia agreed. "When my parents return from India, I wonder how we all will have changed."

"Does it make you sad, even a little?"

Cecilia was not certain she had ever considered the matter in that light. "I suppose it does, Lady Janet," she replied after a moment's thought. "Perhaps this is a lesson to us both: not to dwell in the past and wish for those times again, but to move on and change."

"It's a sobering consideration," Janet said. "Do you ever wish you could do something over?"

"Not really. I like to look ahead." She stood up. "My goodness, you have so much to look forward to!"

"Yes, indeed," Janet said, and Cecilia could hear the amusement in her voice. "Shortbread, drop cakes, and wafers below stairs!"

They smiled at each other with perfect understanding. "Lady Janet, you are going to make Sir Lysander a happy man," she said, keeping her voice low.

"I intend to," Janet replied, "even if he is not as brave as I would like. I love him." She said it softly, with so much tenderness that Cecilia almost felt her breath leave her body. Unable to meet Janet's eyes, because her own were filling with tears, she looked at Lucinda, sleeping so peacefully beside her sister. You are all so fine, she thought. Lord Trevor has no need of a prosy scold; nothing is broken here, not really. He was so wrong.

"Lady Janet," she began carefully, not even sure what she wanted to ask. "Do you ... has Lord Trevor ever kept Christmas here with you?"

Janet thought a moment, a frown on her face. "Not that I recall. No. Never. I wonder what it is that he does?"

"I wish I knew."

Breakfast was a quiet affair. Lord Trevor ate quickly and retreated to the book room, saying something about reviewing his cases. David had to ask him twice if he could join him and continue alphabetizing the files. They left the room together. Lucinda and Janet hurried below stairs, and Cecilia found herself staring out the window toward the manor. She had tried to ask Mrs. Grey casually how the work was going, but the housekeeper just looked away and changed the subject. She had tried again after breakfast, with the same response. She found herself growing more uneasy as the morning passed, and she didn't really know why.

"Miss Ambrose?"

Startled out of her disquietude, she turned around to see

Davy standing there. "Davy! Are you thinking it would be good to go below stairs and check on your sisters' progress? It already smells wonderful, doesn't it?"

To her surprise, he shook his head. To her amazement, he came closer and rested his head against her waist. In a moment she was on her knees before him, her arms tight around him. "My dear, you're missing your mother, aren't you? She'll be here tomorrow."

Davy burrowed as close to her as he could, and she tightened her grip. "Davy, what is it?"

She pulled him away a little so she could see his face, took a deep breath, then pulled him close again. "What's wrong?" she whispered in his ear, trying to sound firm without frightening him.

"It's my uncle," he said finally, the words almost forced out between his tight lips. "I'm afraid."

Cecilia sank down to the floor and pulled him onto her lap. "Oh, Davy, tell me," she ordered, fighting against her own rising tide of panic.

Davy shivered. "Miss Ambrose, he just sits and stares at the case files! I ... I tried to talk to him, but he doesn't seem to hear me! It's as though there is a wall ...." His voice trailed away.

Cecilia ran her hands over his arms, and rubbed his back as he clung to her. "Tell me, my dear," she urged.

He turned his face into her breast, and his words were muffled. "He told me not to look into the files, and I didn't, until this morning." He looked up at her, his eyes huge in his face. "Miss Ambrose, I have never read such things before!" He started to cry.

She held him close, murmuring nonsensicals, humming to him, until his tears subsided. "My dear, you don't know what he does, do you?"

Davy shook his head. "No, but I think it really bothers him."

"I think you are right, Davy." She put her hands on each side of his face and looked into his eyes. "Can you get your coat and mittens?"

He nodded, a question in his eyes.

"We're going outside to get some fresh air." She stood up, keeping Davy close. "Perhaps we can figure out what to do with all that holly you collected yesterday."

The coats were in a closet off the front entrance. She helped Davy with his muffler and made sure his shoes were well buckled, then got into her coat. Mrs. Grey and the cook were below stairs with the girls. She could hear laughter from the kitchen now and then. She tiptoed down the hall to the book room and pressed her ear against the door panel. Nothing.

They left through a side door out of sight of the book-room windows. She did not have a long stride herself, but she had to remind herself to slow down anyway, so Davy could keep up.

"We're not supposed to go to the manor," he reminded her as they hurried along. "Uncle Trevor is afraid we will be hurt while the repairs are going on." He stopped on the path. "He might be angry, Miss Ambrose!"

"I don't know what he will be, Davy, but I want to see the renovations." If a judge and jury had demanded to know why she was so determined, she could not have told them. Some alarm was clanging in her brain. She did not understand it, but she was not about to ignore it one more minute.

On Davy's advice, they approached the manor from the garden terrace. There was only a skiff of snow on the flower beds, which had been cleaned, raked, and prepared for a long Yorkshire winter. All was tidy and organized.

Her parents had done extensive renovations once on their Egyptian villa. She remembered the disorder, the dust, the smell of paint, the sound of saw and hammer. When she opened the door off the terrace and stepped inside with Davy, there was none of that confusion. Nothing. The house was completely silent. Nothing was out of place. She sniffed the air. Only the faintest smell of smoke remained; she couldn't be sure it wasn't just the ordinary smell of a household heated with coal.

Davy stared around him, and took her hand again. "There's nothing wrong."

"No, there isn't," she said, keeping her voice calm, especially when she saw the question in his eyes. "Where are the workers?"

They walked down the hall, holding tight to each other, until they came to the door that led belowstairs. Cecilia took a deep breath and opened it. As soon as she did, they heard voices, the soft slap of cards, and some laughter. She took a firmer grip on the boy's hand, and they walked down the stairs together.

The workers sitting around the table in the servants' hall looked up when she came into the room. The oldest man— he must have been the foreman—smiled at her. "G'day, miss!" he called, the voice of good cheer. "Are you from that dower house?"

She smiled back, even though she wanted to turn and run. "Yes, indeed. I am a teacher for one of the young ladies, and this is David Chase, Viscount Goodhue."

The men put down their cards and got to their feet.

"Is my uncle Trevor playing a joke on us?" Davy asked her.

"Let's ask these men," she said. "Sir, have you been repairing any damage at all?"

The foreman shrugged. "After Lord Trevor sent all the servants off on holiday, we opened up the windows and aired out the place. Watts, over there—perk up, Watts!—cleaned out the pipe behind the Rumford and seated it again, but that's all the place really needed." He scratched his head. "His lordship's a good man, he is. Said he just wanted us to stay here all week, and get paid regular wages."

"Did he ... did he tell you why, precisely?" Cecilia asked.

"I don't usually ask questions like that of the gentry, miss, but he did say something about wanting to keep everyone close together."

He said as much to me, she thought, hoping that his young relatives would discover each other again, if they were in close quarters. "I can understand that," she said.

"Yes, mum, that's what he said," the foreman told her. "This is our last day on the job." He laughed and poked the cardplayer sitting next to him. "Guess we'll have to earn an honest wage next week again!"

The men laughed. The man called Watts spoke up shyly. " 'E's made it a happy Christmas for all of us, miss. You, too, I hope."

"Oh, yes," Cecilia said, wishing she were a better actress. "Lord Trevor is a regular eccentric who likes a good quiz! Good day to you all, and happy Christmas."

They were both quiet on the walk back to the dower house, until Davy finally stopped. "Why would he want us to keep close together?"

"He told me that first night, after you were all in bed, that he was worried that you were all growing apart, and were ungrateful for what you had," she explained. "He had a notion that if you were all together, he could give you what he called a 'prosy lecture' about gratitude." She took his hand, and set him in motion again. "Davy, the people he works with—his clients—are young, and have so little. He helps them all he can, but …." But I don't quite understand this, she thought to herself. He does so much good! *Why* is he so unhappy?

The dower house was still silent when they came inside, but the odors from the kitchen were not to be ignored. Without waiting to stamp off the snow upstairs, she and Davy went down to the kitchen, where his sisters were rolling dough on the marble slab. She watched them a moment, their heads together, laughing. Nothing wrong here, she thought. She looked at Davy, who was reaching for a buttery shortbread.

She noticed that Mrs. Grey was watching her, and she took the housekeeper aside. "Mrs. Grey, there's nothing going on at the manor. Do you know why Lord Trevor is doing this?"

"You weren't to know," the woman declared.

The room was quiet, and she knew the children were listening. The frown was back on Davy's face, and his sisters just looked mystified. "Uncle Trevor's been fooling us," Davy said. "There's nothing wrong with our home."

It took a moment to sink in, then Lady Janet sat down suddenly. "We ... we could have had the Christmas entertainment? And Lysander could have come?"

"I think so, Lady Janet," Cecilia said. "He said he wanted everyone here in close quarters so you could all appreciate each other again." She reached out and touched Lucinda's arm. "But I don't think there ever really was a problem."

She smiled at Janet. "Well, maybe a word or two in the right ear was necessary, but that was a small thing."

"I know I'm glad to be here now," Lucinda said. She put her arm around her sister, then tightened her grip as her face grew serious. "I told Uncle Trevor that very thing this morning, but I'm not sure he heard me."

"I did the same thing in the book room," Davy said. "Told him I missed Mama, but it was all right. He didn't seem to be paying attention."

Davy looked at Cecilia, his eyes filled with sudden knowledge. "Miss Ambrose, he was trying to *fix* us, wasn't he? We're fine, so why isn't he happy?"

It was as though his question were a match struck in a dark room. Cecilia sucked in her breath and sat down on the bench, because her legs felt suddenly like pudding. She pulled Davy close to her. "Oh, my dear, I think he is trying to fix himself."

She knew they would not understand. She also knew she would have to tell them. "Mrs. Grey, would you please leave us and shut the door?"

The housekeeper put her hands on her hips. "I don't take orders from houseguests," she said.

Janet leaped to her feet. "Then you'll take them from me! Do as Miss Ambrose says, and ... and not a word to my uncle!"

Bravo, Janet, Cecilia thought, feeling warmer. When the door closed with a decisive click, she motioned the children closer. "Do you know what your uncle really does? No? I didn't think so." She touched Davy's face. "You have some idea."

He shuddered. "Those files …."

"Your uncle is an advocate for children facing sentencing, deportation, and death."

Janet nodded, and pulled Lucinda closer to her. "We do know a little of that, but not much." She sighed. "I own it has embarrassed me, at times, but I am also proud of him." She looked at her sister. "I think we all are."

"And rightly so, my dear," Cecilia said. "It is hard, ugly work, among those who have no hope." She took a deep breath. "Let me tell you about Jimmy Daw."

She tried to keep the emotion from her voice, but there were tears on her cheeks when she finished. Janet sobbed openly, and Lucinda had turned her face into her sister's sleeve.

Davy spoke first. "Uncle Trevor didn't mean any harm to come to Jimmy Daw."

"Oh, no, no," Cecilia murmured. "He thought he was doing something kind."

"Is Jimmy Daw why he works so hard now?" Lucinda asked, her voice muffled in her sister's dress.

"I am certain of it," she said, with all the conviction of her heart.

"Then why isn't he *happy*?" Davy asked, through his tears. "He does so much good!"

Cecilia stood up, because the question demanded action from her. "Davy, I fear he has never been able to forgive himself for Jimmy's death, in spite of the enormous good he has done since." She perched on the edge of the table and looked at the three upturned faces, each so serious and full of questions. "He probably works hard all year, works constantly, so he can fall asleep and never dream. He probably has no time for anything except his desperate children."

"Father does say that when he and Mama go to London, they can never find a minute of time with Uncle Trevor," Janet said.

"Does he come here for Christmas?"

"Hardly ever," Lucinda replied. She stopped; her eyes grew wider. "He might stay a day or two, but he is always gone well before Christmas Eve. You said Jimmy died on Christmas Eve."

"He did." Cecilia got up again, too restless to sit. "I don't know what your uncle usually does on Christmas Eve, but somehow he must punish himself." She started to stride about the room again, then stopped. "I doubt he was planning to stay, in spite about what he said of his 'prosy lecture,' that he could have delivered and left."

"He was forced to, wasn't he?" Janet said slowly. "When Mama and Papa went to be with Amelia, he had no choice!"

"No, he didn't," Cecilia replied. "I think he used the excuse of the fire to keep everyone close. My dears, I think he *wants* to change now—if not, he would have bolted as soon as I got here—but I think he is afraid to be alone. And that is really why we are crammed so close here." She sat down again, dumbfounded at the burden that one good man could force upon himself.

They were all silent for a long moment. Janet looked at her finally, and Cecilia saw all the pride in her eyes, as well as the fear. "I love my uncle," she said, her voice low but intense. "There is not a better man anywhere, even if people of our rank make fun of him." She smiled, but there was no humor in it. "Even Lysander thinks him a fool for—oh, how did he put it?—'wallowing in scummy waters with the dregs.' My uncle is no fool." Her eyes filled with tears again. "Miss Ambrose, how can we help him?"

She mulled over the question, and then spoke carefully. "I think first that he would be furious if he knew I had told you all this."

"Why did he tell you?" Davy asked.

It was a question she had been asking herself for several days now. She shook her head, and started to say something, when Janet interrupted.

"Because he is in love with Miss Ambrose, you silly nod,"

she told her brother, her voice as matter-of-fact as though she asked the time of day.

Cecilia stared at her in amazement. "How on earth...." Janet shrugged, and then looked at Lucinda, as if seeking confirmation. "We both notice how his eyes follow you around the room, and the way he smiles when he looks at you." She grew serious, but there was still that lurking smile that made her so attractive. "Trust me, Miss Ambrose, I am an expert on these matters."

Cecilia laughed, in spite of herself. "My goodness."

"Do you mind the idea?" Lucinda asked, doubt perfectly visible in her eyes.

Did she mind? Cecilia sat down again and considered the matter, putting it to that scrutiny she usually reserved for scholarship. Did she mind being thought well of by a man whose exploits had been known to her for some time, and whom she had admired for several years, without even knowing him? Her face grew warm as she thought of his grip on her waist as they left the smoky manor in the middle of the night. "He doesn't even know me," she protested weakly.

"As to that, Miss Ambrose, I have been writing him about you," Lucinda said.

"You have *what*?" she asked in amazement.

Her pupil shrugged. "He wanted to know if there was anyone interesting in my school, and I told him about you." She hesitated. "I even painted him a little picture."

"Of me?" she asked quietly. Me with my olive skin and slanted eyes, she thought.

"Of you, my most interesting teacher ever," was Lucinda's equally dignified reply. "He's no ordinary man."

And I am certainly no ordinary English woman, she thought. She reached across the table, took Lucinda's hand, and squeezed it briefly. "You are the most wonderful children."

Janet laughed. "No, we're not! We probably are as selfish and ungrateful as Uncle Trevor imagines. But do you know, we aim to be better." She grew serious and asked again, "How can we help our uncle?"

"Leave him to me," Cecilia said. "I know he does not want you to know about Jimmy Daw, or he would have told you long before now, Janet. How can I get time alone with him?"

Davy was on his feet then. "Lucinda, do you remember how fun it was last Christmas to spend it in the stable?"

"What?" Cecilia asked. "You probably needn't be *that* drastic!"

"You know, Miss Ambrose," Janet said. "There is that legend that on the night of Christ's birth, the animals start to speak." She nudged her brother. "What did Davy do last year but insist that he be allowed to spend the night in the stable! Mama was shocked, but Papa enjoyed the whole thing." She looked at her younger brother and sister. "We will be in the stable. The footman can light a good fire, and we have plenty of blankets."

The other children nodded, and Cecilia could almost touch the relief in the room. Precious ones, she thought, you will do anything to help your uncle, won't you? No, you most certainly do not require fixing. "Very well," she said. "Janet...." She stopped. "Oh, I should be calling you Lady Janet."

"I don't think that matters ... Cecilia," the young woman replied. "I will make arrangements with Mrs. Grey, and we will go to the stables after dinner." She looked at her siblings. "Cecilia, we love him. We hope you can help him because I do believe you love him, too."

They were all quiet that afternoon, soberly putting Christmas treats and cakes into boxes for delivery to other great houses in the neighborhood on Boxing Day, arranging holly on mantelpieces, and getting ready for their parents' return on Christmas. After an hour's fruitless attempt to read in the sitting room, Cecilia went for a walk instead. How sterile the landscape was, with everything shut tight for a long winter. Little snow had fallen yet, but as she started back toward the dower house, it began, small flakes at first and then larger ones.

Soon the late afternoon sky was filled with miniature jewels, set to transform the land and send it to sleep under a blanket of white. She stood in the modest driveway of the dower house and watched the workers leave the manor for the final time. Some of them called happy Christmas to her. She looked at the house again, wondering why it was that the most joyous season of the year should cause such pain in some. With a start, she realized that her preoccupation with Lord Trevor and his personal nightmare had quite driven out her own longing for her family in far-off India. "Tonight, I hope I remember all the wonderful things you taught me," she said out loud. "Especially that God is good and Christmas is more than sweets and gifts."

Before dinner, she went to the book room, squared her shoulders, and knocked on the door. When Lord Trevor did not answer, she opened the door.

He sat probably as he had sat all day, staring at his case files, which Davy had alphabetized and chronologized. Everything was tidy, except for his disordered mind. When she had been standing in the doorway for some time, he looked at her as though for one brief moment he did not recognize her. She thought she saw relief in his eyes, or maybe she only hoped she did.

"Dinner is ready, Lord Trevor," she said quietly. "We hope you will join us."

He shook his head, then deliberately turned around in his chair to face the window. She closed the door, chilled right down to the marrow in her bones.

Dinner was quiet, eaten quickly with small talk that trailed off into long pauses. A letter had come that afternoon from York with the good news that the marquis and marchioness would arrive at Chase Hall in time for dinner tomorrow. "I wish they were here right now," Davy said finally, making no attempt to disguise his fear.

"They'll be here tomorrow," she soothed. "Davy, I promise to take very good care of your uncle."

Her words seemed to reassure them all, and she could only applaud her acting ability, a talent she had not been aware of before this night. After a sweet course that no one ate, Janet rose from the table and calmly invited her younger brother and sister to follow her. Cecilia followed them into the hall, and waited there until they returned from their rooms bundled against the cold.

Janet looked almost cheerful. She tucked her arm through Lucinda's and reached for Davy. "Do you know, this is my last Christmas to be a child," she said to Cecilia. "I will be married in February, and this part of my life will be over." She looked at her siblings. "Lucinda, you will marry someday, and even you, Davy!" He made a face at her, and she laughed softly. "I am lucky, Miss Ambrose, and I *did* need reminding."

"We all do, now and then," Cecilia replied. She opened the door, and kissed each of them as they passed through. "If you get cold, come back inside, of course, but do leave me alone in the book room with your uncle."

'Take good care of him," Lucinda begged.

"I will," she said. "I promise you."

Easier said than done. When the house was quiet, she found a shawl, wrapped it tight around her for courage, and went to the book room. She knocked. When he did not answer, she let herself into the room.

He sat at the desk still. This time there was only one file in front of him. He looked at her and his eyes were dark and troubled. "What are you doing here?" he asked, his voice harsh.

"The children wanted to spend Christmas in the stable," she said. "It's a silly thing."

"I remember when they did that, years ago," he said. "I remember…." Then he looked at the file before him, and he was silent.

Her heart in her throat, she came into the room and around the desk to stand beside him. "Is that Jimmy Daw's file?" she asked.

He put his hand over the name, as though to protect it. She wanted to touch him, to put her arms around his shoulders and press her cheek against his, all the while murmuring something in his ear that he might interpret as comfort. Instead, she moved to the front of the desk again and pulled up a chair.

"He died eleven years ago this night, didn't he?" She kept her voice normal, conversational.

Lord Trevor narrowed his eyes and glared at her. "You know he did. I told you."

"What is it you do on Christmas Eve to remember him?" There.

Silence. "Shouldn't you be in bed, Miss Ambrose?" he asked finally, in a most dismissive tone.

She smiled and leaned forward. "No. It's Christmas Eve, and the children are busy. I think I will just stay here with you, and see what you do to remember Jimmy Daw, because that's what you do, isn't it? You probably plan this all year."

More silence.

"Do you go to church? Read from the Bible? Work on someone else's charts? Visit old friends in the City? Have dinner out with your fellow barristers? Sing Christmas carols? Squeeze in another good work or two?" She stopped, hating the sound of her own rising voice and its relentless questions. She looked him straight in the eye. "Or do you just sit at your desk hating yourself?"

He leaped to his feet, fire in his eyes, and slammed the file onto the table like a truncheon. "I don't need this!"

She looked away, frightened, but held herself completely still in the chair. It was then that she noticed the row of bottles against the wall. My God, she thought, my God. With courage she knew she did not possess, she stood in front of him until they were practically toe to toe. "Or do you try to drink yourself to death, because you failed one little boy?"

He raised his hand and she steadied herself, because she

knew it was going to hurt, considering his size and the look in his eyes. Almost without thinking, she grabbed him around the waist and pulled him close to her in a fierce grip. She closed her eyes and waited for him to send her flying across the room. She tightened her grip on the ties on his waistcoat. All right, she thought, you'll have to pry me off to hurt me.

To her unspeakable relief, the file dropped to the floor and his arms went around her. She released her grip and began to run her hands along his back instead. 'Trevor, it's going to be all right. Really it is,' she murmured.

He began to sob then as he rested his chin on her hair. "I line up a row of bottles and drink my way through Christmas Eve, Christmas, and Boxing Day, Cecilia," he said, when he could speak. "I almost died last Christmas, but damn me if one of the other barristers at the Inn didn't come knocking on Christmas afternoon. I woke up with a surgeon's finger down my throat!" He leaned against her until his weight almost toppled her. "Please stop me! I don't want to die!"

Holding him so close that she could feel his waistcoat buttons against her breast, she understood the enormity of his guilt, as irrational as it seemed to her logical mind. She moved him toward the sofa and sat down. He released her only to sink down beside her and lay his head in her lap. She twitched her shawl off her shoulders, spread it over him, and rested her hand on his hair—did he never comb it, ever?—as he cried. Sitting back, she felt his exhaustion and remorse seeping into her very skin. As he cried and agonized, she had the tiniest inkling of the Gethsemane that her dear foster father spoke of from the pulpit, upon occasion. "Bless your heart," she whispered, "you're atoning for the sins of the world. My dear, no mortal can do that! What's more, it's been done, and you don't have to."

"That's your theology," he managed to gasp, before agony engulfed him again.

"And I am utterly convinced of it, dear sir," she said. Cecilia pushed on his shoulder until he was forced to raise himself and look at her. She kissed his forehead. "Even someone as young as Davy understands that we celebrate Christmas because Christ gave us *hope!* Dear man, you're dragging around chains that He took care of long ago." She kissed him again, even though his face was wet and slimy now. "I really think it's time you stopped."

"But Jimmy's dead!"

It was a lament for the ages, and she felt suddenly as old and tired as he, as though he had communicated the matter into her in a way that was almost intimate. She considered it, and understood her own faith, perhaps for the first time. "Yes, Jimmy Daw is dead," she whispered finally as he lowered himself back to her lap, his arm around her this time. "And you have done more to honor his memory than any other human being. Every child you save is a testimony to your goodness, and a memorial to Jimmy Daw. I know it is. I believe it."

He didn't say anything, but he had stopped crying. She knew he was listening this time. She cleared her throat, and wiped her own eyes with a hand that shook. "May I tell you how we are going to celebrate Christmas Eve next year? We are going to remember all the children you have *saved*. We are going to thank Kind Providence that you have the health and wealth to do this desperately hard work."

"We are?" he asked, his voice no more than a whisper.

"We are," she replied firmly. "You are not going to do it alone ever again."

What am I saying? she asked herself, waiting for the utter foolishness of her declaration to overtake her. When nothing of the kind happened, she bowed her head over his, then rested her cheek against his hair. "You're a good man, Trevor Chase. I even think I love you."

"Cecilia," was all he said, and she smiled, thinking how tired he must be. She could feel his whole body relaxing. After a long time of silence, she moved her legs, and he sat up.

"I believe I will go to bed now," she told him. She stood up and looked at the row of bottles, waiting there still. "Or should I stay?"

He shook his head, and reached for a handkerchief. He blew his nose vigorously. "If you want to open that window and drop them out, I think that would be a wise thing. Old habits, you know."

She knew. She opened the window and did as he said. The first bottle didn't break, but the others did as they landed on each other. She leaned out, then pulled back quickly from the fumes rising over the rosebed. She gathered up her shawl and went to the door. "Good night, and happy Christmas, Trevor," she said, and blew him a kiss.

The house was so quiet. She pulled herself up the stairs, practically hand over hand, and went into the girls' room. The bed looked far more inviting than her own little cot. Since they were in the stable, she shucked off her clothing down to her shimmy and crawled in.

She was nearly asleep when Lord Trevor opened the door, came to the bed, and stood there. "I threw the file on the fire," he said, his voice sounding as uncertain as a small child's.

"Good," she told him, and after only the slightest hesitation, pulled back the blankets.

"Are you certain?" he asked.

"Never more so."

"I don't want to be alone tonight," he told her as he took off his shoes, then started on his waistcoat. "I'm so tired."

"I know you are, but I have to know one more thing. I think you know what it is."

He sat down on the bed, and rested his head in his hands. "I do. I was going to go back to my chambers this year, lock the door, and keep drinking until ...." He stopped, unable to speak.

Cecilia sat up and leaned her head against his back. "My

God, Trevor, my God," she whispered. "What ... what changed your mind?"

"Well, I had to stay here with the children when Hugo and Maria bolted, but even then ...." He turned around and put his arm around her. "Then you came, and I had second thoughts. I didn't plan on falling in love."

"Just like that?"

"Just like that. Are you as skeptical as I am?"

"Probably. But, the bottles in the book room tonight?"

"I don't know if I would have drunk any of them, considering how matters had changed. I suppose I'll never know," he told her as she put her arms around him. "I think I was counting on you to stop me. Thank you from the bottom of my heart, Cecilia."

He lay down beside her and gathered her close. With a sigh, she threw her arm over his chest and rested her head in that nice spot below his collarbone. His hand was warm against her back. Her feet were cold and he flinched a little when she put them on his legs, but then he kissed her neck, and fell asleep.

He was gone in the morning. Cecilia reached out a tentative hand; his side of the bed was still a little warm. She got up and dressed quickly, then hurried downstairs. She heard laughter from the breakfast room, his laughter. She opened the door.

"Lucy, you are telling me that your graceless scamp of a little brother actually stood over by the horses and began to *talk*?" asked Lord Trevor. The picture of relaxation, he slouched negligently in his chair, with his arm along the back of Lucinda's chair.

Janet giggled. "He scared Lucy so bad that she jumped up and stepped in the water bucket the footman had left by the lantern!"

"Did not!"

"Oh, we both saw it!"

Lord Trevor held up both hands. "I've never met more disgraceful children," he scolded, but anyone with even the slightest hearing could have picked out the amusement in his voice. "It's never too late for my prosy lecture. Good morning, Miss Ambrose, how do you do?"

I know my face is red, she thought. "I do well," she replied. "Happy Christmas to you all."

Lord Trevor pushed out a chair with his foot. "Have a seat, my dear Miss Ambrose. I've told my long-suffering relatives all about my silliness next door at the manor. They have agreed that a week in the dower house was not too unpleasant." He smiled at them all. "And now they will move their belongings back, with some help from Mrs. Grey and the footman."

"Mama is coming home today," Davy said.

"I received a letter from Lysander only a few minutes ago," Janet said, holding out a piece of paper. She smiled at Cecilia. "He promises to come as soon as all contagion is gone."

Cecilia poured a cup of tea and sat down, just as the children rose and left the room. Davy even looked back and winked. "Scamp," she murmured under her breath, trying to concentrate on the tea before her, and not on Lord Trevor, who had decided to put his arm on her chair now. In another moment his hand rested on her shoulder, and then his fingers outlined her ear.

"You're making this tea hard to drink," she commented.

"It isn't very good tea, anyway," he told her as he took the cup from her hand and pushed it away. He cleared his throat. "Cecilia—Miss Ambrose—it has certainly come to my attention that I ... er ... uh ... may have compromised you last night."

I love him, she thought, looking at him in his rumpled clothes, with his hair in need of cutting. I wonder why he does not stand closer to his razor, she thought. His eyes were tired, to be sure, but the hopeless look that had been increasing hour by hour on Christmas Eve was gone. She turned in her chair to face him.

"I would say that you certainly did compromise me. How

loud you snore! What do you intend to do about it?"

"What, my snoring?"

She laughed and leaned toward him. He put his hand around her neck, drew her closer, and kissed her forehead.

"I suppose I must make you an offer now, eh?" he asked, the grin not gone from his face.

"I would like that," she told him. "We'll be an odd couple, don't you think?"

"Most certainly. I'm positive there will be doors that will never open to either of us," he replied, without the blink of an eye. "People of my sort will wonder if I have taken leave of my senses to marry Cleopatra herself, and those evangelizing, missionary friends of your parents will assume that you have taken pity on a man desperate for redemption." He kissed her again, his lips lingering this time. "Oh, my goodness. Cecilia, I will be bringing home scum, riffraff, and strays."

"Of course. I'm going to insist that you close your chambers at the Inn and move me into a house on a quiet street where the neighbors are kind and don't mind children," she said, reaching for him this time and rubbing her cheek against his. She felt the tears on his face.

"Miss Deprave is going to be awfully upset when you give your notice," he warned.

She giggled. "Your brother and sister-in-law will probably have a fit when you tell them this afternoon."

He laughed and pulled her onto his lap. "There you are wrong. They'll be so relieved to find a lady in my life that they won't even squeak!"

She tightened her arm around his neck as the fears returned momentarily. "I hope they are not disappointed."

"No one will be disappointed about this except Miss Deprave. Trust me, Cecilia."

"Trust a barrister?" she teased, putting her hands on both sides of his face and kissing him.

"Yes, indeed." His expression was serious then. "Trust me. I trusted you when I told you about Jimmy that second night." He took her hand. "I looked at your lovely face, and some intuition told me I could *say* something finally." He shook his head.

She knew she did not know him well yet, but she could tell he wanted to say something more. "What is it?" she prodded him. "I hardly think, at this point, that there is anything you might be embarrassed to tell me."

He looked at the closed door, then pulled her onto his lap. She sighed and felt completely at home there.

"Before I left London, I made a wish on a star. Is that beyond absurd?"

Resting there with her head against his chest and listening to the regular beating of his heart, she considered the matter. "Teachers are interested in results, dear sir, not absurdities. Did it come true?"

"Oh, my, in spades."

She went to kiss his cheek, but he turned his head and she found his lips instead. "Then I would say your wish came true," she murmured, once she could speak again.

He smiled. "I'm a skeptic still, but I like it."

"I like it, too," she admitted.

"D'ye think you'll still like it thirty or forty years from now?" he asked.

"Only if you're with me." She kissed him again. "Promise?"

"Promise."

No Room at the Inn

⌒

"**M**AMA, ARE WE THERE yet?"

Mary McIntyre smiled, and added another entry to her growing list of what was going to make the single life so comfortable.

"I told you less than fifteen minutes ago that the snow is slowing our progress."

Mary glanced at Agatha Shepard, her seat companion, who was doing her best not to glare at her offspring. I understand totally, Mary thought. She was no more inclined than a child to enjoy creeping along at a snail's pace, through a rapidly developing storm.

She had left Coventry two days earlier, joining the travel of Thomas and Agatha Shepard and their two children from London, who were to spend Christmas in York with Agatha's parents. The elder Shepards—he was a solicitor with Hailey and Tighe—already appeared somewhat tight around the lips when they stopped at her parents' estate. In a whispered aside, Agatha said that Thomas had not made the trip any easier with his deep sighs each time the children insisted upon acting their age.

Mary understood perfectly; she had known Thomas for
years. What was it that his younger brother Joe told her once?
"If people could select their relatives, Thomas would be an
orphan."

As much as she liked Agatha, Mary never would have
chosen the Shepards' company for anything of greater length
than an afternoon's tour of Coventry's wonderful cathedral.
The fates had intervened, and dictated that she be on her way
to Yorkshire. Two weeks ago, her station in life had changed
drastically enough to amuse even the most hardened Greek
god devoted to the workings of fate.

She wished she could pace around the confining carriage and
contemplate the folly of an impulsive gesture, but such exercise
would have to wait. Tommy and Clarice quarreled with each
other, their invective having reached the dreary stages of "Did
not! Did, too!" My head aches, she thought.

They should have stopped for the night in Leeds, even
though they had scarcely passed the noon hour. Agatha's timid
"Thomas, dear, don't you think ..." had been quelled by a fierce
glance from her lord and master.

"My dear Agatha, I pay our coachman an outrageous sum
to be highly proficient," he said. He glared around the carriage,
his eyes resting finally on his squabbling olive branches.
"Agatha, can you not do something about *your* children?" he
asked, before returning to the legal brief in his lap.

We could dangle *you* outside the carriage until you turn blue,
Mary thought. "Thomas, don't you think it odd that we have
not observed a single wheeled vehicle coming from the other
direction in quite some time?" It's worth a try, she thought. Let
us see if I have any credit left with the family solicitor.

She discovered, to her chagrin, that she did not. Not even
bothering to reply, the family solicitor stared at her. She sat
back in embarrassment.

I suppose it is good to know where one stands in the
greater scheme of events, she told herself later, when she

felt like philosophizing. There was a time, Thomas Shepard, when you would have been nodding and bobbing at my least pronouncement, she thought. You would have at least considered my request to stop, and there would have been no withering looks. I think I liked you better when you were obsequious. And *that* is a sad reflection upon me, she decided.

She thought about Colonel Sir Harold Fox, Chief of Commissary Supply, currently serving occupation duty in Belgium. His last letter to her had indicated a season of celebration, now that the Monster was on his way to a seaside location somewhere apart from shipping lanes in the South Atlantic. "My dear, you dance divinely," he had written. "I wish you were here, as we endure no end of balls and routs."

I doubt you wish that now, she told herself. When her father—no, Lord Davy—broke the news to her, she had calmly retreated upstairs and wrote to Sir Harry. He had made her no declaration, but in his last letter, he had hinted broadly that he would be asking her a significant question during his visit home at Christmas. It seemed only fair to alert him that he might not wish to make her an offer.

She sighed, then hoped that Agatha was engaged with her children, and not paying attention. Should I be angry at life's unfairness? she asked herself, then shook her head. Here she sat, fur-lined cloak around her, in a comfortable coach, going to spend Christmas with …. She faltered. With a grandmother I do not even know, who lives on a *farm*, God help me.

They continued another two hours beyond Leeds, with the coachman stopping again and again for no reason that Mary could discern beyond trying to see if he was still on the highway. She knew Agatha was alarmed; even the children were silent, sitting close together now.

Another stop, and then a knock on the carriage door. Thomas pulled his overcoat up around his ears and left the vehicle to stand on the roadway with the coachman, their backs to the carriage. Young Tommy looked at Mary. "I have a pocketful of raisins, and Clarice has a muffin she didn't eat from breakfast this morning," he told her seriously.

Mary reached over to touch his cheek. "I think you are wonderful children," she told him. "How relieved I am to know that because of your providence, we won't starve." He smiled back, at ease now.

Thomas the elder climbed back in the carriage a few minutes later, bringing with him a gust of snow. He took a deep breath. "The coachman advises me that we must seek shelter," he said. "Thank God we are near Edgerly. If the inn there is already full, we will be forced to throw ourselves on my brother's mercy."

Tommy clapped his hands. "Clarice, did you hear that? Uncle Joe!"

"I didn't know Joe lived around here," Mary said.

A long silence followed. When Thomas finally spoke, there was an added formality to his careful choosing of words. "He purchased what I can only, with charity, describe as a real bargain, Miss McIntyre. I tried to make him reconsider, but Joe has ever been stubborn and inconsiderate of the needs of others."

And *you* are not? she thought.

The discussion animated Agatha. "Oh, my dear, it is a wreck!" she confided. "A monstrosity! He bought it for practically pence from a really vulgar mill owner who thought to retire there." She giggled, their plight momentarily forgotten. "I believe the man died of apoplexy after taking possession of the place. Thomas thinks the shock carried him away. The place was too much, even for him!"

A smile played around Thomas's lips. "I told him he'd regret the purchase." He shrugged. "That was four years ago. We haven't heard much from Joe since."

She tried to remember Joseph Shepard, the second son of her father's—no, Lord Davy's—estate steward, which wasn't difficult. She couldn't help smiling at the memory of a tall, handsome man who spent a lot of time in the fields, who was cheerful to a fault, and who seemed not to mind when both she and her little sister Sara fell in love with him. Edgar followed him everywhere, and there was never a cross word. Of course, he was a family servant, she reminded herself. He must be nearly thirty-three or so now, she thought.

The inn at Edgerly proved to be suffering from the same problem experienced many Christmases ago. The innkeeper came out to their carriage to say that he had no room for anyone more. "Of course, you could sit in the taproom," he suggested.

"We would never do that," Thomas snapped.

I wish your father could hear you now, Mary thought, and felt no regret at her own small-mindedness. Funny, but if my choice was for my family to freeze in a carriage, or sit among less renowned folk in a taproom, I would choose the taproom. She smiled. Perhaps I *am* better suited to the common life.

"Well, then," said the innkeeper. "I won't keep you from … uh … whatever it is you think you can do now."

"One thing more," Thomas said. Mary felt her toes curl at his imperious tone. "Are you acquainted with Joseph Shepard?"

"We all know Joe! Are you a friend of his?"

"I am his brother."

"Who would have thought it?" the keep said. "Planning to drop in on him now?"

Thomas glared at him. "My arrangements are my business. Give me directions."

The innkeeper looked inside the carriage, and Mary realized exactly what he was thinking. She had no doubt that if Tom had been unaccompanied, he would have been given directions that would ultimately have landed him somewhere north of St. Petersburg. Mary couldn't resist a smile at the keep, and was rewarded with a wink.

Practically feeling his way like a blind man, the coachman finally stopped before a large house, just as the winter night settled in. The carriage shifted slightly as the coachman left his box and walked around to the door. Thomas stepped down after the coachman dropped the steps. "Agatha, I predict that Joe will open the door. He has probably sent his servants home during the Christmas season. Providing he has any to send home!"

The Shepards chuckled as Mary watched thoughtfully. "I suppose you have retained your regular household in London this week, even though you are not there?" she asked, hoping that the question sounded innocent.

"Of course!" Agatha exclaimed. "The housekeeper will release them for a half day on Christmas. Only think what an excellent time this is for them to clean and scrub."

"Of course," Mary murmured. "Whatever was I thinking?"

The house was close to the gate. Peering through the darkness, Mary could discern no vulgar gargoyles or statues. It appeared to be of ordinary brick, with a magnificent cornice over the door, which even now was opening.

"It *is* Joe himself," Agatha said. "There is probably not a servant on the place."

The carriage door opened, and Joseph Shepard looked around at them, his eyes bright with merriment. "Can it be? Lord bless me, do I see Tommy the Stalwart, and Clarice the Candid? Welcome to Edgerly, my dears."

It felt like a rescue, especially when he held out his arms and his niece and nephew practically leaped into them. Agatha's feeble effort at control—"Children, have you no manners?"—dissolved quickly when he beamed at her, too. "Oh, Joe, thank goodness you're here! I do not know what we would have done."

He only smiled, and then looked at her. "Lady Mary? What a pleasure."

His arms were full of children so he could not help her down. Instead of retreating to the house with his burden, he stood by the carriage while Thomas helped Agatha and then

Mary from the vehicle. He brushed off Agatha's apologies with
a shake of his head, then led the group of them to his house.
Mary still stood by the carriage as the others started up the
narrow walk. The coachman closed the carriage door. "Things
are always a little better when Joe is around," he said, more to
himself than to her.

She started up the walk after the others, when Joe came
toward her. He had deposited the children inside, and he
hurried down the steps to assist her. She did not think she had
seen him in at least eight years, when she was fifteen or so,
but she would have recognized him anywhere. He bore a great
resemblance to his brother; both were taller than average, but
not towering, with dark hair and light eyes. There was one
thing about him that she remembered quite well. She peered
closer, hoping she was not being too obvious, to see if that
great quality remained. To her delight, it did, and she smiled
at him and spoke without thinking. "I was hoping you had not
lost that trick of smiling with your eyes," she said, and held out
her hand.

"It's no trick, Lady Mary," he replied, and he shook her hand.
"It just happens miraculously, especially when I see a lovely
lady. Welcome to my house."

He ushered her in and took her cloak. She looked around in
appreciation, and not a little curiosity. He must have noticed
the look, because he glanced at Thomas and his family toward
the other end of the spacious hallway. "Did Thomas tell you I
was living in a vulgar barn I bought for ten pence to the pound
from a bankrupt mill owner?"

She nodded, shy then.

"All true," he told her. "I wonder why it is he seems
faintly disappointed that the scandalous statues and the red
wallpaper are gone?" He touched her arm. "Perhaps he will
be less disappointed if I tell him that the restoration is only
half complete, and he will be quite inconvenienced in the
unfinished bedchambers. Do you think he will prefer the jade

green wallpaper, or the room where Joshua and I have already stripped the paper?"

She laughed, in spite of herself. "Joshua?" she asked.

"My son. I believe he is belowstairs helping our scullery maid, Abby, cook the sausages." Joe looked at his brother. "Thomas, I trust you have not eaten yet?"

"And where would that have happened?" Thomas asked in irritation. "Even the most miserable inn from Leeds on is full of travelers! Surely you have something less plebian than sausages, brother," Tom continued.

"We were going to cook eggs, too," Joe offered, with no evident apology.

"And toast," Thomas said with sarcasm. Her face red, Agatha tugged at his arm.

"Certainly. What else?"

"Brother, did you dismiss your staff?"

"I did, for a fact," Joe stated. "My housekeeper has a sister in Waverly, and she enjoys her company around the holiday. Ditto for my cook, of course. The two maids—they are sisters—informed me that their older brother is home from the war. I couldn't turn them down."

"I call it amazingly thoughtless of you!"

Mary stared at Thomas and curled her hand into a fist. Surprised at herself, she looked down, then hoped that no one had noticed. She was almost afraid to look at the brothers. The angry words seemed to hang in the air between them. "Thomas, I am certain your brother had no any idea that we were all going to descend on him," she said.

Thomas turned to glare at her. "*Miss* McIntyre, this is a matter between me and my brother," he snapped. "I'll thank you to stay out of it."

Joseph Shepard spoke quickly. "Thomas, have some charity. It's Christmas." He smiled at Mary. "Lady Mary, if you don't mind what I am certain amounts to delving deeper into low company than you ever intended, you might want to help

Joshua belowstairs. I know that you are a game goer, and we need more sausages." He gestured down the hall. "It's through that door. I'll sort out some sleeping arrangements."

"Certainly," she said, grateful to flee the scene.

The servants' hall was empty, so she followed her nose into the kitchen, where two children stood by a modern Rumford stove. The little boy with the apron about his middle who poked at sausages sizzling in the pan was obviously Joshua. The young girl who cracked eggs into a bowl must be Abby. She felt their scrutiny, but also felt it was unencumbered by the tension that was so heavy upstairs.

"Hello, my dears," she said. "My name is Mary McIntyre. I think I'm going to be a Christmas guest. Joshua, your uncle Thomas and his family are upstairs. Your father says there will be a few more people for dinner."

"Good," he replied. "We like company." He smiled at her. It was Joe Shepard's slow smile, but without any other resemblance to the originator of it. As the boy put more sausages in the pan, she wished his uncle Thomas could have appeared belowstairs to witness real courtesy.

Mary rolled up her sleeves and placed herself at the service of the scullery maid, who shyly asked for more eggs, and showed her how to crack them. When she admired the way Abby whisked the eggs around in the bowl and told her so, the child blushed and ducked her head. "She's a little shy, Miss McIntyre," Joshua said.

Joe Shepard came downstairs when the next batch of sausages was cooking. He helped Abby pour the eggs into a pan. "You see what good hands I am in, Miss McIntyre," he said, "even if my own brother thinks I am a barbarian without redemption." He leaned against the table. "I think I offended Agatha's maid."

"Never a difficult task," Mary murmured. "Did you dare suggest that if she wanted a can of hot water that she come belowstairs to get it?"

"How did you know?" he asked. "She insists that the 'tween stairs maid bring it up to her." He looked at his son. "Josh, do we need a 'tween stairs maid?"

"I could take her a can," he suggested.

"No, no. Let's see if she comes for one. Some tea, Miss McIntyre?"

"Delighted." She accepted the cup from him. "It appears that your brother has told you of my fall from grace, since you are no longer calling me Lady Mary." He nodded, and took a sip from his own cup. "I don't understand it, though." He glanced at the children. "Lord and Lady Davy took you in when you were a baby, and only decided just before Christmas to tell you that it was all a *mistake*? My Lord, that's gruesome." He took another sip. "I could almost think it cruel."

He was saying exactly what she felt, and until that moment, had refused to acknowledge. He must have noticed the tears in her eyes, because he gave her his handkerchief. "I didn't mean to make you do that," he told her. "Just another example of my barbarism, I suppose. Forgive me, Miss McIntyre. You can explain this a little later, if you wish. I don't want to pry, but I'm used to thinking of you as Lady Mary."

"I'm used to hearing it," she said. She had to change the subject. "Is Joshua's mother away?"

"Farther than any of us like. She died three years ago," he said. "I don't know if you even knew I had married, but she was a fine woman, a widow with a little boy."

"Josh?"

"Yes." She could see nothing but pride in his eyes as he regarded the boy at the Rumford. "Isn't he a fine one? I'm a lucky man, despite it all."

She looked at Joshua, and back at Joe Shepard. I think I have stumbled onto quite a family, she thought. "He's certainly good with sausages." It wasn't what she wanted to say, but it seemed the right thing, particularly since Agatha's maid was stomping down the stairs now. Joe got up to help her.

As the maid, her back rigid, snatched the can from Joe and started for the door, he called after her, "Miss, could you tell the others that dinner will be ready soon?"

She turned around, her expression awful. "I do not announce meals!"

"Good Lord, what was I thinking?" Joe said.

"Papa, why is she so unpleasant?" Joshua asked when the maid slammed the door.

"Happen someone forgot to tell her it was Christmas," he replied. He bowed elaborately to Abby. "My dear Miss Abigail, if you and Miss McIntyre will go upstairs and lay the table, we will bring up dinner. Do I ask too much?"

Abby laughed out loud. As Mary got up to follow her, she noticed the look that Joe and Joshua exchanged.

"She came to us from a workhouse in September," Joe explained. "I do believe this is the first time she has laughed, isn't it, Josh?"

The boy nodded. "Maybe she finds the maid amusing."

"I know I do," Joe said.

"Come, miss," Abby called from the top of the stairs.

"Right away, my dear!" She turned to Joe. "Did she stay here with you this Christmas because she has nowhere else to go?"

"Precisely."

I have nowhere to go, either, Mary thought as she went upstairs. And then surprisingly, may I stay here, too?

THE THOUGHT PERSISTED THROUGH dinner, even as she carried on a perfectly amiable conversation with Agatha, and everyone tried to ignore Thomas's elaborate, rude silence. His eye on his father, Tommy began a cautious conversation with Joshua, which quickly flourished into a real discussion about the merits of good English marbles over the multicolored ones from Poland.

Joe had placed Abby next to him. He kept his arm along the back of her chair in a protective gesture that Mary found gratifying. Joe carried on a light conversation about the changes underway in his house, but offered no apologies for the inconvenience.

"Did you construct that beautiful cornice over the front door?" Mary asked.

"I designed it, but I hired a stonemason for the work." He beamed at her in the way that she remembered. "Familiar to you, Miss McIntyre?"

"Indeed, yes," she replied. "I seem to recall a similar cornice over the door that leads onto the terrace at Denton."

"I always liked it," he said. He looked at his brother. "Tom, d'ye remember when we weeded the flower beds below the terrace?"

Thomas turned red in the face. "I see no point in remembering those days."

"Pity, considering what an enjoyable childhood we had," Joseph said. He turned his attention to Mary. "I remember a time you and Lady Sara got in trouble for coming to help us weed. How is she, by the way? And Lord Milthorpe?"

"Really, Joseph," Thomas said in a low voice. "I already told you that Miss McIntyre has had a change in her circumstances."

"True, brother. What I know of Miss McIntyre, unless she has changed drastically, is that she couldn't possibly forget the people she was raised with, unlike some," Joseph replied, his voice calm, but full of steel. "I trust they are well?"

Oh, bravo, Mary thought. "Lady Sara has got herself engaged to a marquess from Kent. Our … her parents have gone there this Christmas to renew their acquaintance with the family. Edgar—Lord Milthorpe—is desperately disappointed that the wars are over and he cannot pester Papa … Lord Davy … to purchase a commission."

"Do give Lady Sara my congratulations when next you see her," Joseph said as his brother rose. "Thomas, I have no brandy, so I can offer you no inducement to stay at table. Agatha, I do not even have a whist table."

"That's all right," she replied. "I believe I will see the children to bed now."

"Oh, Mama!" Tommy protested. "I would very much like to see Joshua's marbles. Oh, please, Papa. It is nearly Christmas!"

Thomas opened his mouth and closed it again. He sighed and went to the door of the breakfast room.

Joseph looked at his brother. "Is that someone at the door? Could it be Father Christmas, or is someone else lost? Tom, could you answer the door?"

"I do not answer doors in strange establishments," Tom snapped. In another moment they heard him on the stairs.

"I doubt he would carry hot water, either," Abby said. She gasped, and stared at Agatha Shepard. "Begging your pardon, ma'am."

Agatha rose to the occasion, to Mary's relief. "I believe you are right, child."

Mary followed Joseph into the main hall and stood watching as he opened the door on a couple considerably shorter than he was, and older by several decades. "Frank! We are saved!" cried the woman.

Mary turned away so no one would hear her laugh.

They were Frank and Myrtle King of Sheffield, and the driver of their hired post chaise, with a tale to tell of crowded inns, surly keeps, full houses along the route, and snow with no end in sight. "I can pay you for yer hospitality, sir," Mr. King declared as Joe tried to help him with his overcoat. "Nothing cheap about me! I'm assistant manager at the Butler Ironworks in Sheffield."

His eyes bright, Joseph turned to Mary. "Miss McIntyre, meet the Kings. I do believe we are all going to spend Christmas together."

THE KINGS HAD NO objections to going belowstairs; Mary could see how uncomfortable they seemed, just standing in the hallway of Joe's magnificent bargain house. Frank repeated his earnest desire to pay for their accommodations, and Myrtle just looked worried and chewed on her lip.

While Mary stirred the eggs this time, and Joseph cooked more sausage, the coachman led his team around behind the house to unhitch them, and came inside again to report that he was going to be fine in the stables with the Shepards' coachman. He tucked away the first order of sausage and eggs, and assured them that they would both come inside for breakfast, come morning.

Provided there is anything left to eat, Mary thought as she poured more eggs into the pan on the Rumford. To her amusement, Joe nudged her shoulder. "We have a full pantry, Miss McIntyre," he told her. "Too bad there is not a cook among us."

"There is, sir," Myrtle declared. "There's nothing I can't cook."

"Then you are an angel sent from heaven, Mrs. King," Joseph declared.

She giggled. "It appears to me that you and your missus shouldn't have dismissed your entire staff for the holiday. Were you planning to go away, too, but for the snow?"

"I did dismiss my staff, Mrs. King," Joseph said. "As for going away, no. Miss McIntyre is an old acquaintance, and she and my brother and his family were stranded by the weather, too." He turned back to the stove long enough to fork the sausages around and allow his own high color to diminish, to Mary's glee.

"Orphans in the storm, eh?" Mrs. King said.

"Precisely. We will be in your debt, madam, if you would cook for the duration of this unpleasant weather. I have a scullery maid, and Mary here is a willing accomplice." He laughed. "Did I say accomplice? Did I mean apprentice?"

"I think you meant accomplice, Joe," Mary said, without a qualm that their relationship seemed to have changed with the use of her first name. "Mrs. King, I do hope you like your eggs scrambled. It is my sole accomplishment. Mr. King?"

She made no objection to Joe's suggestion, an hour later, that they adjourn to the bookroom upstairs with a bottle between them. The Kings were safely tucked in belowstairs in the housekeeper's room. Abby had retired to the room that she shared belowstairs with the absent maids, and Mary promised to join her there later.

"Of course, more properly you should be upstairs, but the only room left unoccupied has two sawhorses and everything else draped in Holland covers. Joshua thinks it is spooky, and so do I."

"I am certain I will be quite comfortable in the maids' room. Is that brandy? Didn't you tell your brother you had none?"

"Hold your glass steady, Mary," he said as he tipped in a generous amount. "It is smuggler's brandy and my last remaining bottle. I doubt that I will drink it anymore now that the sea lanes are open and the challenge is gone." He took an appreciative swallow of his own glass. "Chateau du Monde, 1790. Would *you* waste that year on a prig?"

She propped her feet up on the hassock between the chairs. "Never!"

Joe took another sip, and leaned back. "I'll tell you my troubles, but you first, Mary, unless it makes you desperately unhappy. I want to know what happened to you. It's not every day that an earl's daughter turns into plain Mary McIntyre."

She settled herself comfortably into the chair, wondering if the late Mrs. Shepard had used the chair before her. If that was the case, Joe's wife must have been about her size, because it suited her own frame. "I don't suppose it is, Joe," she agreed. "My mother—oh, I know she is Lady Davy, but please, you won't mind if I call her my mother, will you? She still feels amazingly like my mother."

Joe was silent. She looked at him, startled to see tears in his eyes. She touched his arm. "Joe, don't feel sorry for me."

"Call me a fool, then."

"Never," she declared. "Mama never let me read those ladies' novels. You know, the ones where the scullery maid turns out to be an earl's daughter? Isn't that what happens in those dreadful books? Who can believe such nonsense?"

"I can assure you that *my* scullery maid isn't an earl's daughter. Where do authors get those stupid notions?" He took another drink.

She held out her glass for more. "My case is the precise opposite of a bad novel. Papa and Mama had been married for several years, with no issue in sight, apparently."

"It happens." He held up his own glass to the firelight. "I know."

"Mama had a modiste who called herself Clare La Salle, and claimed to be a French émigrée."

"That's glamorous enough for a bad novel," Joseph said. "I take it that Clare was not her real name."

"No, indeed. Apparently Clare found herself in an interesting condition."

"Any idea who the father was?"

Mary giggled. "I think I am drunking ... drinking ... this too fast."

"You can't be too careful with smuggler's brandy, my dear," Joseph said.

"I don't think he was a marquess or a viscount," she said. "Clare came to Mama in desperation, and she and my parents hatched a scheme. You can imagine the rest."

"What happened to Clare?"

"She was so obliging as to die when I was born, apparently. Mama had retired to Denton, so no one knew I wasn't really hers," Mary said. "What could interfere now? Mama found herself in an interesting condition later, and Sara was born. And then Edgar." She tipped back the glass and drained it.

"You're not supposed to drink it so fast. A sip here, a sip there." Joe set the bottle on the floor between them. He settled lower in his chair. "So Lady Mary, daughter of the Earl of Denton, spent a blissful childhood of privilege, completely ignorant of her actual origins." He looked at her. "Do you think it was just two weeks ago that they had second thoughts about their philanthropy?"

She shook her head. "As I reflect on it now, I think not."

"You never had a come-out, did you?"

My stars, she thought, you were mindful of such a thing? "No, I never did. I am surprised that you were ever aware of it, though."

He took another sip. "Don't think me presumptuous when I say this, but your family was a choice topic of conversation in our cottage." He shrugged. "I expect this is true of any large estate."

She digested what he said, and could not deny the probable truth of it. The reverse gave her some pause; at no point in her life had she ever been interested in those belowstairs. "We never spoke of you, sir," she said honestly.

"A candid statement," he said. "I appreciate your honesty." He took another sip. "I wager that you do not remember the first time I could have come to your attention."

"You would lose, sir. I remember it quite well."

"What?"

"Let me tell you here that Sara and I both fell in love with you when we were little. We decided you were quite the nicest person on the whole estate."

"My blushes."

"You rescued me from an apple tree when I was five," she said, enjoying the embarrassment on his face. "As I recall, Thomas put me there on a dare from the goose girl."

"That was it," he said, and took a deep drink. "I trust you and Lady Sara survived your infatuation?"

"I think we did. But you know, I never thanked you for rescuing me."

"You weren't supposed to."

"Then I thank you now."

They were both quiet. Mary smiled and looked into the

flames. "Now that I think of it, by the time for my come-out, my parents were likely coming to realize the deception they were practicing on those of their rank regarding my ... my unsuitability."

"I say, sod'um all, Mary."

She gasped. "Joe, your language!"

He leaned across the space between them, his eyes merry. "Sod them, I say. You always were the most interesting of the lot, Mary McIntyre."

"Joe, you're mizzled."

"No, I'm stinking. I do this often enough to know." He winked at her. "Did you want a come-out?"

"No. I like to dance, but I have no patience for fashion—can you imagine how my real mother is spinning in her grave? Idle chat bores me." She rested her chin on her hand. "Joe, I'm going to miss Denton." The tears slid down her face then. She had never drunk herself into this state before, and she decided to blame the brandy.

Joe seemed not to mind. He didn't harrumph and walk around in great agitation, as Lord Davy had when she cried after his terrible news to her. He regarded her for a moment. "What finally brought the matter to a head? Who connected the McIntyres with Clare La Salle?"

She took another drink. "It was a Bow Street Runner, of all things. Mrs. McIntyre—she would be my real grandmother—had long mourned that wayward daughter. After some years, she contacted the Bow Street Runners. After considerable time and much perseverance, they connected her missing daughter to Clare La Salle through one of London's houses of fashion. They found me less than a month ago," she concluded simply.

She took a deep breath. "Mama couldn't face me. Papa told me the whole story. He offered me an annuity that Hailey and Tighe drew up. I ... I signed it and left the room Mary McIntyre."

"Damn them all, Mary."

"No," she said quickly, startled at his vehemence. "I have an income that most of England would envy, and all my faculties. It could have been much worse." The silence from the other chair told her quite eloquently that Joseph Shepard did not agree. She folded her hands in her lap and felt greatly tired. "I will miss them all. Lord Davy thinks it best that I quietly fade from the scene. No family needs scandal. I have … had a suitor, Colonel Sir Harold Fox. Perhaps you remember him?"

"Yes, indeed. A tall fellow who rides his horses too hard."

"Does he? I have written him a letter laying the whole matter before him. We shall see what he chooses to do. Rides his horses too hard, eh?"

Joe laughed. "Sod him, too, Mary."

She joined in his laughter, feeling immeasurably better. "Your turn, Joe," she said when she quit laughing. "Why are you and Tom so out of sorts?"

She thought he was disinclined to reply at all, considering the lengthy silence. Or it may have been only a few moments. The brandy had enveloped her in a cocoon that either shut out time, or let it through in odd spurts.

"I hope this won't offend you," he began finally.

"No one else has been concerned about offending me lately," she reminded him.

"Your father—well, Lord Davy—is a misguided philanthropist, I do believe."

Two weeks ago she would have disputed with him, but not now. "My father was his estate steward, as you know," he went on. "One day he told my father that he wanted to educate Tom and me. You know, send us to university, give us a leg up. Lord Davy paid Tom's charges at the University of London, and he became a solicitor."

"But not a barrister? Does that bother him?"

He looked at her with some appreciation. "Bravo, Mary! Poor Tom. No matter how fine his patronage, no one would ever call Tom, the son of a steward, to the bar."

She thought a minute. "I really don't recall seeing Thomas much at Denton, after he went to university."

"Try never. We weren't good enough," he said, and took another drink. "He never came around. Think of it, Mary: he was too good to visit the steward's cottage, and will never be good enough for an invitation to Denton Hall. Poor man, poor man."

She mulled it over. "There is a certain irony to this conversation, Joe," she said after some thought. "Tom goes up in society, but never quite high enough. I go down …"

"… but you will always be a lady, no matter what your former relatives do to you. He may just resent you, too, Mary." He was starting to mumble now from the brandy. "You're in good company, because he resents me, too."

"Because you didn't go to university? Obviously you turned down the same offer from Lord Davy."

"Oh, but I did go to university. I did well, even though it bored me beyond belief. It is …. It is worse than that."

She stared at him, feeling definitely muddled from all that brandy. She closed her eyes, and after a moment, the matter became quite clear. She laughed.

Joe watched her appreciatively. "Figure it out?"

"Joe, you'll have to tell me what you do for a living, I suppose," she said.

"I am a lowly grain broker, but by damn, I am a hell of a businessman." He smiled. "Despite my lofty education!" He started to laugh again, which made him look suspiciously at the glass in his hand. He set it on the floor. "I decided to do what I like. Every spring I visit farms and estates in Yorkshire, make predictions, and give them an offer on their crops. It is called dealing in futures, and I am good."

She clapped her hands, delighted at his good fortune. "I can hardly imagine more lowly commerce."

"Thank you! I have considered developing a side line in the bone and hide business, just to spite Thomas." He grinned.

"Imagine how I would stink! If I were to turn up at his London house, Thomas would probably fall on his knife."

She watched him, not flinching at his scrutiny, even as she felt her whole body grow warm. Sir Harry never looked at me like that, she thought. I should go to bed. There was one more matter; the brandy fogging her brain reminded her. "Let us see how this tallies: Thomas is unhappy because he will never scale the heights he feels he deserves, and he resents your success. I have seen my hopes of a lifetime dashed. What about you? You said earlier that you spend too much time doing just this."

It sounded so blunt that she wished she had not spoken, especially when he avoided her gaze. "I miss my wife," he said, just as bluntly. "She was a grand woman, although I daresay Tom would have thought her common, had he ever met her."

"Would I have liked her?" Mary asked.

"You would have loved her," he replied promptly. "You remind me of her a little: same dark hair, eyes almost black, quiet, capable. Tall, for a woman. I like looking women in the eye." He reached out to touch her leg, then pulled his hand back. She held her breath, not moving, not wanting to break whatever spell he was under. He took one deep breath and then another, and she could tell the Chateau du Monde had worked on him. "Maybe I was even thinking of you when I met her, Lady Mary. Or maybe I am thinking of her now when I see you. Or maybe I am drunk beyond redemption tonight." He shook his head. "I will be sober in the morning and regret this conversation."

"I do hope not, Joe," she said quietly. She was silent then, as spent as he was. After a moment, she moved her legs away from the hassock, then gathered herself together enough to stand. Her head seemed miles away from her feet. "I am relieved that is your last bottle of Chateau Whatever-it-is."

He chuckled, and struggled to his feet. "Let me help you down those stairs, Mary McIntyre. I would feel wretched if you landed in a heap in the servants' hall."

She could think of no objection as he put his arm around her waist and pulled her arm around his. By hanging onto the wall, then clutching the banister, he got her to the door of the maids' room.

"Are you all right now?" he whispered. He turned his head. "Lord, can Frank King ever snore. Unless that is Myrtle."

They laughed softly together, his head close to hers. He leaned on her, and she thought for a moment that he was asleep. For no discernible reason—considering that her brain was starting to hum—she thought of Christmas. "Joe," she whispered. "Do you and Joshua not really celebrate the season?"

"I never quite know what to do," he replied.

"Have you any holiday decorations?"

"Melissa had quite a few, but I do not know that either of us are up to those yet."

"Any others?" He was leaning on her quite heavily now.

"There may be a box belonging to the defunct owner of this palace," he said. "Probably vulgar and destined to set off Thomas. Oh, do find them!" He laughed.

She put her hand over his mouth to silence him, and he kissed her palm, his eyes closed, then it was her wrist. His head was so close that she couldn't think of a reason not to kiss his cheek. "I think I will see what Mrs. King and I can do about Christmas," she murmured, "considering that we are snowbound."

He pulled her very close then, giving her brandy-soaked brain the opportunity to consider the feel of him in some explicit detail. They were about the same height. When she turned her face to look at him—so close he was out of focus— kissing him seemed the only thing to do that made any sense.

He must have been of similar mind. He kissed her back, one hand tugging insistently at her hair, the other caressing her back in a way that made her sigh through his kiss.

Mr. King stopped snoring. Joe released his grip on her hair

when she pulled away, and regarded her sleepily, but with no apology.

"Do you think we woke him up?" Joe asked quietly, his voice a little strange.

"I don't know," she whispered back. "Lord, I hope not."

Joe touched his forehead to hers. "Good night, Mary," he said. "In future, have a care who you drink with. Yorkshire is full of scoundrels and skirt raisers."

She went quietly into the maids' room, closed the door, and leaned against it. She laughed when she heard him stumble on the steps, then held her breath, hoping he would not plunge to the bottom. Scoundrels and skirt raisers? she asked herself. Hmm.

She woke to the sound of someone screaming in her ear. Someone well schooled in torture must have placed weights on her eyes, because they refused to respond. She managed to open one eye.

Mrs. King, her eyes kindly, stood beside her bed. She held a tall glass.

"Someone was screaming," Mary gasped.

"Oh, no, dearie," she said. "I just said good morning." She lowered her voice when Mary winced. "Abby was concerned about you, but I told her you just didn't get enough sleep last night, Miss McIntyre."

And caroused well beyond my limit, Mary thought. "Thank you for that, Mrs. King," she whispered. "I believe I will never drink brandy with Mr. Shepard again."

The older woman put her hand to her mouth. "He said exactly the same thing this morning, my dear, when he prepared this little concoction for you."

"Do sit down, Mrs. King," she said, and pressed both hands to her head. "If I told you that I generally drink only lemonade, and take nothing stronger than sherry, upon occasion, you would probably call me a prevaricator."

Mrs. King did laugh then. "Of course I would not! My dear,

I rather think that we shall lay the blame at Mr. Shepard's door. He *is* a persuasive gentleman, isn't he?" She leaned forward and held out the glass. "Do you wish this, my dear?"

Mary eyed the glass with disfavor. "It's so … black," she said. "What is in it?"

"He made me promise not to look, but he left the treacle can on the table."

"Oh, Lord, I am being punished for all my sins," Mary said with a sigh and reached for the glass. Her stomach heaved at the first tentative sip. Here I am, only a few days from my old life at Denton, and I have already yielded to dissipation, she thought. She took a deep breath and drank the brew, then slowly slid back into the mattress.

"He said I was to wait a half hour and then bring you porridge, well sugared."

"I will be dead before then!"

To her amazement, she was not. She lay as still as she could, wondering at the sounds around her. After a moment, she understood why everything sounded strange: she had never heard a house at work from the ground up. In the world she had just left, servants were silent and invisible, the kitchen far away. She listened to Mr. King talking, and heard Joe Shepard laugh at something he said. Chairs scraped against the floor, pans rattled. Mrs. King must have opened the oven door, because the fragrance of cinnamon drifted right under the door.

She looked around. The maids' room was tidy and attractive, with lace curtains, a substantial bureau, and a smaller bed for Abby. The furniture was old and shabby. She knew it must have come belowstairs after its usefulness ended abovestairs, but it was polished and clean. I wonder if servants' quarters are this nice at Denton, she mused.

She thought then about her own establishment. Lord Davy had promised to provide her with a house anywhere she chose to live. Although he had not stated the obvious, she knew he would be more comfortable if she were far away. "After a while, people will forget," he had told her. To her enduring sorrow, he had not even flinched as he threw away her entire life. *And your questionable background will not be an embarrassment* was unspoken but real.

I wonder if Canada would be far enough for Papa, she thought, or even the United States. I am an educated lady of comfortable means, but what am I to *do* with myself? I need never work. If Sir Harry does not choose to pursue his interest in me, I am unlikely to marry within that sphere I thought I was born to inhabit. And who of another class would have me? Joe Shepard, you are right: Lord Davy was a misguided philanthropist.

When the snow stopped, they would continue their journey, and she would be deposited at the home of her real grandmother, the woman who had begun the search that ruined her life. "A farm in Yorkshire," she said out loud. Joe, you may be at home on the farms, but I am not, she concluded. I have nothing in common with anyone on a farm.

She got out of bed slowly. Dressing taxed her sorely. Her own lady's maid had left her employ a week ago when the gory news of her mistress's changed social status filtered down to the servants at Denton. When Genevieve had approached her, eyes downcast, and said that she had found a position on a neighboring estate, she learned another bitter lesson: servants cared about social niceties. Genevieve knew that working for the illegitimate daughter of a modiste was not a stepping-stone to advancement.

She took only a few minutes with her hair. Brushing it made her wince, but it was an easy matter to twist it into a knot and know she did not have to worry overmuch that it was tidy. In a rare burst of candor—he was a reticent man—Sir Harry had told her once that he liked her hair *en deshabille*. Well, you should see me today, Harry, she thought.

What she saw in the mirror surprised her. Her cheeks were rosy, and her eyes even seemed to smile back at her, despite the late night and the brandy. Suspecting that her lot today was to scrabble among boxes for holiday decorations, she had put on her simplest dress, a dark green wool with nothing to recommend it beyond the elegant way it hung. At least I won't frighten small children, she told herself as she left the room.

She had hoped that Joe would not be belowstairs, but there he still sat, chopping nut meats on a cutting board. Please don't apologize to me for last night, she thought suddenly, and felt the color rise to her face. Let me think that you enjoyed the kiss as much as I did, and that you wanted to tell me your story, as you wanted to hear mine.

She held her breath as he tipped the knife at her. "Good morning, Mary McIntyre," he said. "Did the magic potion work?"

"I am ambulatory," she said, "That, of itself, is a prodigious feat."

He nodded and returned to the work at hand. "I believe Mrs. King has some porridge for you. Do take these nut meats to her, and then come back, will you? I have all manner of schemes, and you have agreed to be an accomplice, as I recall." He funneled the chopped nuts into a bowl and handed it to her. "If she has any cinnamon buns left, could you bring me another one?"

She smiled at him and went into the kitchen, where Mrs. King presided at the table, rolling out dough while Abby stood by with a biscuit cutter and a look of deep concentration on her face. Clarice hovered close by the bowls of sugar colored green, red, and yellow. "We are making stars, Miss McIntyre," she announced. "And then ivy leaves?" she asked, looking at Mrs. King, who nodded.

"Mrs. King, I believe you are a gift from heaven," Mary said. She set down the bowl of nut meats. "I believe I am to find a bowl of porridge, and there is a request for another cinnamon bun, if such a thing is available."

Mrs. King took the porridge from the warming shelf. "It

already has plenty of sugar, and here is the cream, dearie." She touched Mary's cheek. "You look fit enough."

"I feel delicate," Mary said with a laugh. "Only think: I already know what my New Year's resolution will be!"

Mrs. King leaned toward her, and looked at the little girls before she spoke in a conspiratorial whisper. "You have to beware of even the best men, Miss McIntyre." She straightened up. "Not but what your own mother has not already told you that."

No, she did not, Mary thought. If someone had given my mother that warning, or at least, if she had heeded it, perhaps I would not be here at all. Then she thought of Lady Davy, and her cautions about fortune hunters, which was hardly a concern now. "She warned me, Mrs. King," Mary said. "I intend to be extremely prudent in the new year!"

She handed Joe his cinnamon bun, sat down at the table, and stared at the porridge for a long enough moment to feel Joe's eyes on her.

"It goes down smoother than you think, Mary," he said.

She picked up the spoon, frowned at it, then took a bite. He is right, she thought as she swallowed a spoonful, and another. "Who would have thought porridge is an antidote to brandy?" she murmured. "The things I am learning."

She felt nearly human by the time she finished. She pushed back the bowl, and looked at Mr. King, who had been watching her with a twinkle in his eye. I am in excellent company, she thought suddenly, and the feeling was as warm as last night's brandy. "Mr. King, I know that Joe and I are both feeling some remorse at chaining your sweet wife to the Rumford, and here you are, orphans of the storm."

She stopped, embarrassed with herself, wondering why she had impulsively included herself with Joe Shepard so brashly, as though they had conferred on the matter, as though they were closer than mere acquaintances. She looked down in confusion, and up into Joe's eyes.

"That is precisely what I have been saying to Frank," he said. "We should be ashamed of ourselves for kidnapping the Kings, and setting you at hard labor in the kitchen." He looked at his half-finished cinnamon bun. "Yet I must temper my remorse with vast appreciation of your wife's culinary abilities." He picked up the bun. "You have fallen among thieves, but we are benevolent thieves, eh, Mary?"

And there he was, continuing her own odd fiction. Do we want to belong together? she asked herself. Is there something about this season that demands that we gather our dear ones close, even if we must invent them? She knew without any question that she wanted to continue the deception, if that was what it was; more than that, she *needed* to.

"I agree completely, Joe," she said quietly. "Mr. King, we are in your debt."

To her complete and utter astonishment—and to Joe's, too, apparently, because his stare was as astounded as hers—Mr. King began to cry. As she sat paralyzed, unsure of what to do, tears rolled down the little man's face.

"I'm sure we did not wish to…" Joe began, and stopped, obviously at a loss.

Mr. King fumbled in his waistcoat for a handkerchief and blew his nose into it vigorously, even as the tears continued to course down his cheeks. "What you must think of me …" he said, but could not continue.

Mary sat in stupefied silence for a moment, then reached across the table to Mr. King. "Sir, please tell us what we have done! We would not for the world upset you."

Her words seemed to gather him together. He looked at the kitchen door. "It's not you two," he managed to say finally. "I have to tell you. You have to know." He gestured toward the door that led to the stairs. "Myrtle mustn't see me like this."

Without a word, they rose to follow him across the room, moving quietly because he was on tiptoe. As she looked at Joe, her eyes filled with questions; he took her hand, then tucked her close to him.

With the door shut, the three of them sat on the stairs leading to the main floor. It was a narrow space. Mr. King filled one of the lower steps, and she and Joe sat close together above him, their legs touching. Joe put his arm around her to give himself room.

Mr. King wiped his eyes again. "I'm an old fool," he said apologetically. "I want you to know that in ten years, this is my happiest Christmas."

"But, sir ..." Mary said. "We don't understand."

He kept his voice low. "Fifteen years ago, our only child ran away. Myrtle had many plans for him, but they quarreled, and he left home at Christmastime." He tucked his handkerchief in his waistcoat. "We looked everywhere, sent out the Runners, even, put advertisements in every broadside and newspaper in England. Nothing." He shrugged. "We thought maybe he shipped out on an East India merchant vessel, or took the king's shilling." He looked away. "We followed every possible lead to its source."

"Nothing?" Joe asked. "You never heard of him again?"

Mr. King shook his head. "Not a line, not a visit. I thought Myrtle would run mad from it all, and truth to tell, she did for a while."

"Poor woman," Mary said, and felt her own tears prickle her eyelids. Joe tightened his arm around her, and she gradually relaxed into his embrace.

"Those were hard years," Mr. King said. "After five or six years, Myrtle seemed to come back to herself again." He sighed, as though the memory still carried too much weight. "Except for this: every year near Christmas, she looks at me and says, 'Frank, it's time to seek David.'" He spread out his hands. "And we do. For nearly ten years we've done just that. We set out from Sheffield with a post chaise and driver."

"What ... what do you do?" Mary asked.

"We pick a route and drive from place to place, spend the night in various inns, ask if anyone has seen David King. Myrtle has a miniature, but it is fifteen years old now. One inn after another, until finally she looks at me and says, 'Frank, take me home.' " He shook his head. "He would be thirty-five now, but I don't even know what he looks like anymore, or even if he is alive."

Mary felt her throat constrict. What a fool I am for imagining that I have been given the cruelest load to carry, she thought. "Where were you going this year?"

"Myrtle got it in her head that we should go to Scarborough and drive along the coast up to the Tyne. 'Maybe he's on one of them coal lighters what ships from Newcastle,' she's thinking, and who am I to tell her 'No, dear woman'?"

"You're a good man, Mr. King," Joe said, his voice soft.

"I love Myrtle," he replied simply. "We're all we have."

Mary took a deep breath. "You're stranded here now, and this is better?"

She was relieved to see the pleasure come into his eyes again. Mr. King pocketed his handkerchief this time. "It is, by a long chalk, miss! You see how busy she is. She's going to make Christmas biscuits and buns with the little girls. There will be a whacking great roast going in the oven as soon as I get back in the kitchen to help her lift it. Wait until you taste her Yorkshire pudding!" He reached up to take Joe's hand. "Thank'ee, sir, for giving us a room when there was no room anywhere else."

It was Joe's turn to be silent. Mary leaned forward. "Oh, Mr. King, he's pleased to do it. I think Joe is a great host." She laughed. "Didn't he let me drink up all his smugglers' brandy last night? I think we have *all* stumbled onto a good pasture."

She had struck the right note. Mr. King laughed softly, his hand to his mouth. "I have to tell you, Mr. Shepard, Myrtle was nearly in a rare state, thinking that you and little Josh were doomed to eat sausage and eggs all through the holidays. 'It's not fitting, Mr. King,' she told me, 'especially since his cook left this full larder. Thank God we have come to the rescue.'" He held out his hand. "Do you understand my debt now?"

"I do," Joe said. "And you understand mine, as well." He smiled. "Mr. King, you had better help your charming wife with that roast. I like to eat at six o'clock. Does she stir in all those little bits of burned meat and fat into her gravy?"

"She does, indeed!" Mr. King declared. He stood up. "I do not know when she will tell me it's time to go home, but I know you will keep her busy until then."

"You can depend upon it, sir."

With a nod in her direction, Mr. King left the stairs and went into the servants' hall again, closing the door quietly behind him. Joe stayed where he was, his arm around Mary. He tightened his grip on her. When he spoke, she could tell how carefully he was choosing his words. "Do you know, sometimes I feel sorry for myself."

"You, too?"

They looked at each other. "Did you ever see two more certifiable idiots?" he asked her.

"Not to my knowledge, Joe," she replied, and let him pull her to her feet on the narrow stairs. She dusted off her skirts. "Did you find me some garish decorations?"

"I did, indeed." He started up the stairs. "They proved to be a major disappointment in one respect."

"Oh?"

"They are not nearly as vulgar as I had hoped. I do not think they will cause my dear brother any distress at all."

"That *is* a disappointment. By the way, where is your brother?"

Joe sighed. "He asked me where the mail coach stops, and walked there to see if the road is open. He says he is expecting correspondence from his firm." He shook his head. "Too bad that a man cannot just enjoy a hiatus from work. I always do."

He took her down the hall to what was eventually going to become the library, when the plastering on the ceiling was finished. When she stopped, he looked up at the ceiling with her. "The former owner had several well-bosomed nymphs doing scurrilous things around that central curlicue," Joe said, pointing up to the bare spot. "I didn't want questions from Joshua, so I am replacing them with more acceptable fruit and leaves."

"Coward," she teased.

"Wait until you are the parent of an inquisitive eight-year-old, my dear," he said.

"That is unlikely in the extreme," she told him as she opened up one of the boxes and pulled out a red silk garland.

"Oh? Your children are going to go from age seven to nine, and skip eight altogether?" he asked, pulling out another garland.

She laughed. "Joe, you don't seriously think any men of my acquaintance are going to queue up to marry a woman of such questionable background. Even one with two thousand a year?"

He surprised her by touching her cheek. "I will tell you what I think, Mary McIntyre. I think you need to enlarge your circle of friends."

"You are probably right." What had seemed just right last night seemed too close this morning, but she made no move to back away from him. You would think you wanted him to kiss you again, she scolded herself.

She wasn't sure if she was relieved or chagrined when he patted her cheek and went to the door. "I'm off to find my son and nephew and go hunt for the wild greenery. Can you decorate a wreath or two? I'll ask Mr. King to put a discreet nail over the mantel in the sitting room and another on the front door." He stood in the doorway a moment. "It may be time for Joe and his boy to consider Christmas again."

"A capital notion, sir," she told him. A few moments later, she heard him calling the boys. Why is it that more than one boy sounds like a *herd*, she thought. There was laughter, and then a door slammed. A few minutes later, Agatha Shepard stood in the library doorway, smiling at her. "Could you use some help, Mary?"

More than you know, she thought. Please take my mind off the molehills I am rapidly turning into mountains. "I am under orders from your brother-in-law to create some Christmas." She knew her face was rosy, so she looked into the box of decorations. "What a relief to know this is not a forlorn hope, my dear. I do believe our late mill owner had some notions of a proper Christmas. Look at this beautiful garland."

By the time the boys returned, red-cheeked and shedding snow, Agatha was positioning the last star burst on the window while Mary observed its hanging from the arm of the sofa. "Mama!" Tommy shouted. "Look! Joe says we are holly experts!"

The boys carried a holly wreath between them. "Father tied it for us, but we arranged the holly," Josh said. He looked at Mary. "He said you were to be the final arbiter, whatever that is."

Mary helped the boys carry the wreath to the box of decorations. "It's marvelous, Joshua. If we tie this red bow to the top, it will answer perfectly here over the fireplace."

"See there, Josh, I knew she would know just what else it needed."

She hung the wreath, then turned around to smile at Joe, who held a larger wreath shaped from pine boughs. "And this for the front door?" she asked.

"Yes, indeed, after you and Agatha give it the magic touch." He looked at the room. "Boys, I believe the ladies were busy while we stalked the greenery." He touched his son's shoulder. "Perhaps you and Thomas can convince Mrs. King that you are in the final stages of starvation. She seems like a humane woman." He looked at Agatha, and must have noticed something in her expression. "Do let Tommy have lunch belowstairs. I would not feel right in asking Mrs. King to serve us upstairs. She is my guest, too."

"Mama, please!" Tommy begged. "I know Clarice has been belowstairs making Christmas treats. We could smell them the moment we opened the front door!"

"You may go belowstairs, Tommy," Agatha said quietly. "These are special circumstances." She turned to her brother-in-law. "Thank you for asking, Joe."

He hugged her, and waved the boys off. "My dear sister, loan your shawl to Mary. I need someone to make certain I do not hang this wreath cockeyed."

Mary stopped him long enough to twine a gilt cord through the boughs and tie it in a bow at the bottom. Agatha secured some smaller star bursts scavenged from the bits and pieces remaining in the box, then threw her shawl around Mary's shoulders. "I will go belowstairs and see what wonders Mrs. King has created."

He was still chuckling when he hung the wreath on the front door. "Mary, you must feel sorry for Thomas. He thought he was marrying a proper lady, only to find that she enjoys putting up her own decorations and will probably be rolling out dough when we go belowstairs. He will accuse me of ruining his efforts to be what he is not. Too bad there was no room for *him* at the inn. All right, Mary, what do you think?"

I think that sometimes philanthropy is sadly misdirected, she told herself as she walked backward toward the front gate, her eyes on the wreath. "Move the wreath a little to the left. A little more. There. Excellent."

To her gratification, Joe walked down the path toward her, then turned around for his own look. "You didn't trust me?" she teased.

"I trust you completely," he replied. "I am just wondering what you would think if we painted the trim white. Would that look right against the brick?"

She glanced sideways at him, but his attention was on the

façade of his house. You are doing it again, she thought. You are including me in your decisions, as though I were in residence at this place. Dear, lonely man, are you even aware of it? "Yes, by all means," she said firmly. "And if you can arrange for a cat to nap in one of those windows this summer, that would be the final touch. Oh, flower boxes, too."

"Consider it done, madam. Pansies or roses?"

"Joe, you don't put roses in flower boxes!"

"Pansies, then."

She looked around her at all the snow. Mr. King had shoveled the walks earlier, but there was no getting away from winter's cold and stark trees and branches, with only the idle leaf still clinging. Not a bird flew overhead. "Joe, you speak of pansies and cats in windows," she said softly, "and here we are in December."

He took her arm through his. "I told you last night that I deal in futures, Mary. And excuse me, but you're the one who mentioned the cat. Do you deal in futures, too?"

"Perhaps it's time I did," she replied, her voice soft. How do I do it? I wish I were not afraid, she thought. She wanted to ask Joe about the courage to carry on when things didn't turn out as planned, but there was Thomas walking up the middle of the road, which had been cleared by a crew from the workhouse.

"Tom, the roads are still open behind us, I gather," he said. "Is that a newspaper?"

Tom held it out to him. "There will be a road crew through here by nightfall. Apparently the road to York will be cleared by tomorrow afternoon, or sooner."

"Any mail for you?"

Tom shook his head, but handed a letter to Mary. "It appears that Colonel Sir Harry Fox is in the country. Let us hope this is good news."

She took the letter, which had been addressed several times, as it went from Denton, then to Haverford, Kent, where Lord and Lady Davy had gone for Christmas, to her as-yet unknown grandmother's farm. "I assured the coach driver that I was your solicitor, and would see that you got your letter," Tom said. "I thought I would need to give a blood oath. What a suspicious man!"

"Just doing his job, brother," Joe said serenely. "Perhaps you and I can go to the house and wrangle over whether you must have luncheon upstairs or downstairs, and leave Mary to her correspondence. You are welcome to use my bookroom."

She watched them walk away, already in lively conversation. Poor Joe! Here he had thought to spend a quiet holiday with his son, eating eggs and sausage, and savoring the last of his smugglers' brandy. The only guests with any merit at all are the Kings, she thought. I drank up his brandy and cried, and his own brother is too proud to eat belowstairs. Thank the Lord that we can at least choose our friends.

Sir Harry had posted the letter from London, probably from the family town residence, a particularly magnificent row house in the best square. She had been there on several occasions, the last during a celebration of Wellington's victory in Belgium, when he had danced more than three dances with her, and, face red enough to match his uniform, had declared that she was the finest lady present. After asking Lord Davy's permission, he had corresponded with her through the fall, telling her nothing of interest, because she did not find troop movements or glum Frenchmen to her taste.

In the bookroom, she opened the letter, took a deep breath, and starting reading. When she was finished, she was too astounded to do anything but stare into the fire, ashamed that she had ever written Sir Harry Fox.

She looked up. Someone knocked on the door, but she made no motion to speak or rise to open the door.

"Dearie, don't you want something to eat?"

It was Mrs. King. She got up quickly and opened the door. "Mrs. King, you did not need to do this," she protested as the woman came into the bookroom with a tray.

"That's precisely what Joe said, but I told him I wanted to, and was he going to stop an old woman?"

Mary made herself smile.

"Now, sit back down there and I will set this tray beside you. There, now. May I pour you some tea?"

She started to cry, unable to help herself, helpless to do anything except hold out the letter. Mrs. King's face filled with concern. She closed the door, poured a cup of tea, and sat down, then handed Mary her handkerchief. "You cry until you feel better, dearie, and then you will drink this," she ordered.

Mary sobbed into the handkerchief. Mrs. King settled herself on the arm of the chair and rested her hand on Mary's back. Mary wiped her eyes, blew her nose, and leaned against the other woman, grateful for the comfort, but missing Lady Davy—the woman she would always think of as her mother—with every fiber of her heart.

"Joe told me about your difficulties, dearie," Mrs. King said.

"I think the entire world must know of them, Mrs. King," she said. "I am glad he told you. I would not have you think I am a habitual watering pot."

"I think you're rather a charming lady, and I know that Joe agrees with me," Mrs. King said firmly. "But this is bad news, isn't it? Mr. Shepard—Thomas—is even downstairs walking up and down, hoping that you have good news."

Mary looked down at the letter that she still held. "I suppose he would call this good news, then. Sir Harry has agreed to pay his addresses to me." She thought of Mrs. King's own trials, and tried to hide the bitterness in her words, even as she knew she failed. "He claims that he will not reproach me with my ignominious birth, should we decide to form an alliance." She held out the letter again. "Mrs. King, he has asked all his relatives what they think, and they are united in their opposition to me!" She leaned back and closed her eyes as shame washed over her. "There are probably men taking wagers at White's on what will be the outcome of this sorry tale!"

"And still Sir Harry persists?" Mrs. King asked.

"I suppose he does," Mary said quietly. "Mrs. King, I do not love him. I never have." She turned in her chair for a better look at the woman. "I have come with the Shepards this Christmas because they are to leave me with a grandmother I have never met … on a farm! Sir Harry is my last chance to remain in the social circle in which I was raised." She rested her cheek against Mrs. King's comforting bulk. "Am I too proud?"

Mrs. King's answer was not slow in coming. "P'raps a little, my dear, but if you do not love this fellow, marrying him would be a worse folly than pride." She laughed softly. "I think there are worse fates than farms. Didn't Joe say you had enough income to do what you want, should the farm prove unsatisfactory?"

"It's true," she agreed. She folded the letter, then looked at Mrs. King, who was regarding her with warmth and surprising affection, considering the shortness of their acquaintance. She took her hand. "It's hard to change, isn't it? I mean, I could have gone along all my life as the daughter of Lord Davy, but now the matter is different, and I must change, whether I wish it or not. Mrs. King, I do not know if I am brave enough."

She stopped then, noting the faraway look in the woman's eyes, and the sorrow she saw there. "Here I am complaining about what must seem to be a small matter to you," she said. "Do forgive me."

Mrs. King gave her a little shake. "It is not a small matter! It is your life."

She considered that, and in another moment took a sip of tea. "This will upset Thomas more than you can imagine. He places such emphasis on class and quality." She stood up. "You say everyone is belowstairs?"

Mrs. King nodded. "Thomas is there on sufferance, but Mrs. Shepard seems content to decorate Abby's batch of Christmas stars."

"And Joe?"

"He and Mr. King are playing backgammon."

"Are we a strange gathering, Mrs. King?" she asked. "I suppose that other than Joe and Joshua, none of us are where we really want to be."

Mrs. King rose. "I am not so certain about that, my dear. Are you?"

She could think of no reply that would not involve a blush.

The two of them went down the stairs. Mrs. King gave her a little push when she reached the bottom and stood there, the letter in her hand. Thomas's eyes lighted up. "Do you have good news, Mary?" he asked.

"That may depend on what you consider good news," she replied, and handed him the letter. "Here. I wish you and Joe would read it."

With a nod to Mr. King, Joe got up from the game-board and sat beside his brother, who had spread out the letter on the table. She watched them both as they read, Thomas becoming more animated by the paragraph, and Joseph more subdued. How different they are, she thought, but how different they had always been.

When he finished reading, Thomas looked at her in triumph. "There you are, Mary!" He smiled at his wife, who was dusting the last of the biscuit dough with sugar. "She need not leave her sphere, Agatha." He shrugged. "It may take a year or two before you are received in the best houses again, Mary, but what is that? People forget."

Mary looked at Joe, who finished reading and sat back, his face a perfect blank. He stared at the letter, then picked it up. " '... no matter how disgusting the whole affair is to sensible people, the sort I wish to associate with, I will never reproach you with your ignominious birth,' " he read out loud. "Mary, he is irresistible."

Ignoring his brother, Thomas took her hand. "Mary, you are most fortunate. The road is clear south of us. Any letter you write will reach Sir Harry in a mere day or two."

Joe grabbed the letter. Without a word he crumbled it into a tight ball. "Thomas, I am not sure I even know you anymore," he said, his voice filled with emotion. "You would have Mary McIntyre, this little lady we watched grow up at Denton, pawn her dignity for a crumb or two? I am surprised at you."

Thomas stared at him and his face grew red. Mouths open, Tommy and Joshua had stopped their game of jackstraws. Abby held the rolling pin suspended over another wad of dough. Agatha dabbled her fingers nervously in the sugar. On the other hand, Frank King appeared to be enjoying the drama before him. His eyes were bright as he looked from one to another.

"Joseph, Mary is no lady anymore," Thomas said. "But you are no gentleman."

Oh, God, Mary thought, and felt her face grow white. The brothers glared at each other. Clarice was already in tears, her face pressed against her mother. What has happened here, Mary thought in the silence that seemed to grow more huge by the second. If ever there were unwanted guests, we have met and exceeded the criteria. She knew that she could not please both men. No matter what she said, it would be wrong to someone, and she would offend people she never wished ill.

Her footsteps seemed so loud as she walked the length of the room and stood between the brothers. "You are probably right, Tom. I will write Sir Harry immediately."

"Thank God," Thomas said, his relief nearly palpable.

"I will assure him that even though I am grateful for the honor I *think* he is doing me, I chose not to further the alliance," she concluded.

"My God, Mary, do you *know* what you are saying?" Thomas gasped. "Do you seriously believe you will ever get another offer as good as Sir Harry?"

For the first time that day, or maybe even since Lord Davy had ruined her hopes two weeks ago, she felt curiously free.

"Thomas, Sir Harry is a boring windbag. You can't honestly think he would ever let me forget my origin."

"But he is so magnanimous!" Thomas exclaimed.

"To trample my feelings?" she asked. "I think not. Honestly, Thomas, I believe I would rather … rather … slop hogs and … and … oh, heavens … milk cows at Muncie Farm than endure life with a man who thought I was common!" She gave him a little push. "How unkind you are to call me common! A woman is only common when the people around her tell her that she is. And I am not."

Mary looked around her, noting the expressions of wounded reproach on Agatha's and Tom's faces. Mr. King winked at her, and she smiled back. To her confusion, Joseph was regarding her with what appeared to be amusement. I should be grateful someone considers this imbroglio humorous, she thought with some asperity. In fairness, he is entitled to think what he chooses. Imagine how glad he will be when the road is open.

"Joe, may I use your bookroom again to write that letter?" she asked.

"Of course." His expression had not changed. "Did you say Muncie Farm?"

"I did."

"But your name is McIntyre."

"Yes. From what I gather, the modiste's mother was widowed not long after her daughter ran away and later remarried. I gather I am still a McIntyre, though. You have heard of Muncie Farm?"

"I have. In fact, Thomas, rather than be any hindrance to you when you are able to bolt my vulgar establishment, I can transport Mary to Muncie Farm. I could give you directions, but I can easily take her there." He bowed to them all. "And now, I have some work to do in my shop. Josh? You may come, and Tommy, too. Use my bookroom as long as you need it, Mary." He bowed again. "Mrs. King, I look forward to dinner at six o'clock."

Mary returned to the bookroom with an appetite. Mrs. King's meal, though cold now, took the edge off her hunger quite nicely. She thought she would have to use up reams of paper to find the right words of regret for Sir Harry, but one draft sufficed. After all, Lady Davy had taught her to regard brevity as the best antidote for unreturned love, and quite the safest route. Poor Sir Harry, she thought. You will miss me for a while, perhaps, but I suspect that your paramount emotion will resolve itself into vast relief. Humming to herself, she sealed the letter and set it aside for a brisk walk tomorrow to the inn to mail it.

"Silly," she said out loud. "Tomorrow is Christmas. It can wait for the day after."

After a little more thought, and a long time gazing out the window, she took out another sheet of paper and wrote a letter to Lady Davy. It proved more difficult to write, because she found herself flooded with wonderful memories of her childhood. She knew down to her stockings that she would miss Denton, and her brother and sister, and even more, the quiet, lovely woman who had chosen to take her in, keep her from an orphanage or workhouse, and raise her. If events had not fallen out as Mary desired, it was not a matter to cause great distress now. She chose to remember the best parts. She decided then that she would write Lady Davy at least once each year, whether Lord Davy wanted her to, or not. Perhaps a time would come when she would be invited home.

She did feel tears well in her eyes as she remembered how many of her mother's acquaintances had called her the very image of Lady Davy. I suppose we see what we choose to see, she thought, then rested her chin in her hand. I hope Thomas can see that someday. Joe already seems to understand.

By dinner, the workhouse road crew was shoveling in front of the house. Thomas and Agatha had decided to take dinner upstairs, to Mary's chagrin and Joe's irritation. Mrs. King only laughed and assured him that the entertainment the Shepards had provided far outweighed any inconvenience. "Abby and I will take them food. If it is cold, well, that's the price for being better than the rest of us." She put her arm around Mary. "If they want seconds, they can come downstairs. It is Christmas Eve, after all, and Mr. King and I are on holiday. Dearie, you lay the table here."

Mrs. King's roast beef was the perfect combination of exterior crust and interior pink tenderness. Abby glowed with pleasure when Mrs. King pointed out that the scullery maid had made the Yorkshire pudding. "I may have directed it, dearies, but I think the secret is in the touch, and not the telling. Mr. King, don't be hoarding the gravy at your end of the table!"

The coachmen joined them, coming into the servants hall snow-covered from helping the road crew. "We met a mail coach coming from York, so the highway is open now," the Shepards' coachman told them as he reached for the roast beef. He jostled the King's driver. "We can all be on our way."

Mary could not help noticing the worried look that Mr. King directed at his wife, who was helping Abby with the gravy. Her heart went out to him as she imagined what it must be like to wonder every Christmas when the melancholy would strike her, and how long she would struggle with it. She leaned toward Joe, and spoke softly. "I wonder, do you suppose a parent ever recovers from the loss of a child through an angry word, or a thoughtless statement?"

He shook his head, and rested his hand on Joshua's head. "It doesn't even have to be your own child, Mary, to fear such a disaster. I pray it never happens to me."

She sat there in the warm dining hall, surrounded by people talking, spoons clinking on dishes, wonderful kitchen smells, and fully realized what he was saying to her. I have a grandmother at a place called Muncie Farm, she thought with an emotion akin to wonder. She has been looking for me. Me! Not to shame me with my shaky background, but to *find* me, because I am all that remains of her daughter. I have been dreading this, when I should be welcoming the chance to put someone's mind at rest. It is a blessing ever to be denied the Kings, I fear, and I nearly passed it by. God forgive me.

"You know where Muncie Farm is?" she asked Joe.

He nodded and ruffled Joshua's hair. "We could take you there tomorrow."

"Then you may do it," she said, and took the bowl of gravy from the Kings' coachman, "*after* we have Christmas dinner here with the Kings."

Thomas and Agatha did not invite her to attend Christmas Eve services with them at St. Boniface, which troubled her not at all. There would have been nothing comfortable or even remotely rejuvenating in celebrating the birth of a Peacemaker with people who chose so deliberately to divide. When Joe told the Kings that indeed there was a Methodist establishment in town—although not the better part of town, and certainly not close to St. Boniface—she demurred again. She had heard much about Methodism and the enthusiastic choirs that it seemed to produce, but Abby was accompanying the Kings. She wanted that kindly couple to give the scullery maid their undivided attention.

"What do you generally do on Christmas Eve?" she asked Joe, while they were washing dishes. (Joe had insisted that Mrs. King did not need to do dishes, and Mrs. King had not objected too long.)

"What do we do, Josh?" he asked his son, who sat on a stool, drying plates.

"We read Luke Two, because it talks about shepherds, I think," Josh said. "Then we watch for the carolers." He looked at his father. "Will there be carolers this year?"

"I rather doubt it, son, considering the depth of the snow."

"Do you feed them sausage and eggs after they sing?" Mary teased.

"I will have you know, I make an excellent wassail," Joe replied. He laughed and flipped his son with the drying towel.

"The secret to living here is to maintain low expectations."

When the other guests had left the house—the Shepards by carriage and the Kings on foot—Joe and Joshua made wassail. They carried it outside to the road crew, which was beginning work now on the side streets of the village, now that the main thoroughfare was open for travel. As she watched from the sitting room window, a steady flow of traffic worked its way in both directions, coaches full of travelers anxious to be home by Christmas, or failing that, Boxing Day.

She thought she would find the house lonely, but she did not. She took her copy of *Pamela* into the bookroom, made herself comfortable in the chair where she already fit, and began to read.

As she read, she gradually realized that she was waiting for the sound of Joe returning with Joshua, and then the Kings coming back, probably to sit belowstairs, drink tea, and chat. At peace with herself, she understood the gift of small pleasures. It warmed her heart as no other gift possibly could, during this season of anxiety for her. She smiled when she heard them finally, realizing with a quick intake of breath that she was as guilty as Joe of thinking and speaking as though she were part of the family. We have to belong to someone, don't we? she asked herself. If we don't, then life is just days on a calendar.

She closed the novel when they came into the bookroom, bringing with them a rush of cold, and the fragrance of butter and spices. Joe carried a pitcher and a plate, and Josh dangled the cups by their handles. "We had a little wassail left, and Father purloined the biscuits from belowstairs," Josh said as he sat down beside her on the hassock. He held out a cup while Joseph poured, and handed it to her. "Father says I am to read Luke Two all by myself this year, but if I get stopped on a word or two, he will help me."

Joe handed him the Bible and opened it to the Book of St. Luke before he sat down with a sigh and stretched his long legs toward the fire. He closed his eyes while Joshua read about governors, and taxes, and travelers, and no room. Mary watched his handsome profile and felt some slight envy at the length of his eyelashes. This is a restful man, she thought, not someone tightly wound who is never satisfied. She wondered what he was like in spring and summer, when his life in the fields and among the grain brokers probably kept him in motion from early light until after dark. Did he become irritable then, restless like his brother? She decided no, that Joseph Shepard was too wise for that.

" 'And there were in the same country shepherds abiding in the field, keeping watch over their flock by night.' " Joshua had moved closer to the fire to see better, his finger pointing out the line. He leaned against his father's legs.

As she watched him, Joe opened his eyes and looked at her. He smiled and reached across the space between them to take her hand and hold it firmly, his fingers intertwined in hers. She almost had to remind herself to breathe. You keep watch over your own little flock, don't you, sir, she thought. You even care about your unexpected guests. It was a wild notion, but she even dared to think that he had been caring for her for years, in his own way. She tried to dismiss the notion as patently ridiculous, but as he continued to hold her hand, she found herself unable to believe otherwise.

He released her hand when Joshua finished, and took his dead wife's son on his lap, holding him close. "Well, Josh, we have almost rubbed through another year," he said, his voice low and soothing. "What do you say we go for another one?"

Joshua nodded. Mary had to smile as she realized this must be a tradition with them.

"What about you, Mary? Will you go for another one?" Joe asked her suddenly.

"I ... I do believe I will," she said. Even if it means things do not turn out as we wish, some hopes are dashed, and the future looks a bit uncertain, she added to herself. "We are all dealing in futures, eh?" she asked.

He reached for her hand again. He held it until he heard the Kings returning, when he got up to become the perfect host, and carry his son to bed. When he returned to the bookroom, she was standing by the window, admiring the snow that the moonlight had turned into a crystal path. He stood beside her, not touching her in any way, but somehow filling her completely with his presence. When he spoke, it was not what she expected; it was more.

"I loved Melissa," he told her, his eyes on the snow. "I have to tell you that in some measure, I think I loved her because she reminded me of you." He glanced at her quickly, then looked outside again. "I'm not completely sure, but it is my suspicion. I ... I've never admitted this to myself, so you are the first to hear it."

He took her hand, raised it to his lips, and kissed it. "I am quite sober tonight, Mary McIntyre, so I will say Happy Christmas to you, and let it go at that for now." He shook his head and laughed softly. "Oh, bother it, I would be a fool to waste such a celebratory occasion." He kissed her cheek, gave her a wink, and left the room. In a moment she heard him whistling in the hall.

THE SHEPARDS LEFT AS early as they could in the morning, Thomas just happy to be away, and Agatha shaking her head and apologizing for the rush, but wouldn't it be grand to be in York with grandparents before the day was entirely gone? Of the two, Mary had to admit that Thomas's attitude, though more overt, at least had the virtue of honesty. Joe must have felt the same way. As they stood in the driveway and saw the Shepards off, he turned to Mary. "My brother is honest, even when he says nothing."

Joe declared that his Christmas gift to the Kings was breakfast. "Mary and I will cook eggs and sausage for *you*, my dears." He winked at Mary. "And do I see some presents on the table? That will be the reward for eating my cooking."

By keeping back two presents she had ordained earlier for Thomas and Clarice, Mary had gifts for the children: a sewing basket with a small hoop and embroidery thread for Abby, and a book with blank pages for Joshua. "This is your journal for 1816," she told him. "And let us pray it is a more peaceful year than 1815."

"It usually is in Edgerly," he assured her, which made Joseph look away and cough into his napkin.

Mr. and Mrs. King presented both children with aprons, Abby's of pale pink muslin that had probably been cut down from one of Mrs. King's traveling dresses, and Josh's of canvas, which turned out to be a prelude for his present from his father of carpenter tools. "I saw what 'e was giving you yesterday, lad. Every man needs his own carpenter's apron," Mr. King said.

Nothing would do then but they must all troop out to Joseph's workshop to see the bench Joe had made for Joshua that did not require a box to reach, and the tidy row of tools with smooth grips right for an eight-year-old's hand. While they were there, Joe pointed to a hinged box held tight in a vice. "That is for you, Mary," he told her, and his face reddened a little when he glanced at the Kings. "I will have it done by Twelfth Night and bring it to you at Muncie Farm." He smiled at her. "Provided you are still there. I was thinking of painting it pale green, with a brass lock, unless you have a better idea."

She shook her head, unable to trust her voice. She thought of the presents she had received from Lord and Lady Davy through the years, not one of which had been made by hand. "I ... I ... wish I had something for you," she stammered when she could talk.

Mrs. King was merciful enough to distract them all by throwing up her hands and admonishing Abby because she was faster on her feet to rush back to the kitchen and remove the sponge cake from the Rumford before it turned into char. Mary followed quickly enough herself, happy to leave the men in the workshop, comparing notes on the construction of a miter box.

When crisis, agony, and certain doom had been averted belowstairs, Mary went to the maids' room to pack, a simple task, considering that she had worn her plainest dresses of the entire Christmas season. The coachman had removed her luggage from the old carriage that traveled with the Shepards, and the sheer magnitude of it caused her to blink and wonder what her grandmother at Muncie Farm would think of such extravagance. *Does a woman really need all this?* she asked herself, wondering why she had ever thought it so important. *I should have left some of my hats at Denton with Sara.*

They ate Christmas dinner when the noon bells tolled in Edgerly, a charming tradition reserved for Christmas and Easter. Mr. King had been pleased to offer grace, and did his Methodist best with enough enthusiasm and longevity to make Joshua begin to squirm, and Mrs. King finally whisper to him that the food was getting cold, and what was worse than a shivering Christmas goose?

Mary knew she had never eaten a better meal anywhere. She was asking for Joe to pass the stuffing when Mrs. King suddenly set down her fork and stood up. "Mr. King, I think it is time for us to go," she announced, her face calm, but her eyes tormented. "Don't we have to look for David? Won't he wonder where we are?"

"I am certain of it, my dear," her husband said. He rose and gently pressed her back down to her seat. "We will finish this wonderful dinner that you have made, and then we will be on our way to Scarborough."

To Mary's amazement, Abby burst into loud sobs. She covered her face with her Christmas apron and cried into it. "I don't want you to go, Mrs. King," she cried, getting up from the table to run from the room.

Before she could leave, Mrs. King was on her feet and clutching the child to her ample belly. There was nothing vague in her eyes now, nothing tentative in her gesture. She hugged the sobbing girl, crooning something soft. Mr. King seemed to be transfixed by this unexpected turn of events. He looked at Joe; the glance that passed between them was as easy to read as headlines on a broadside.

"I just had a thought, Mrs. King," Joe began. "Tell me how you feel about it. Hush, now, Abby! You may want to hear this, too." He propped his elbows on the table and rested his chin in his hands. "Abby's a grand girl in the kitchen with the pots and pans, but did you see how she handled that rolling pin yesterday?" He shook his head. "I'm not entirely certain, but it is possible that when my cook returns tomorrow, she just might be jealous of Abby. Where will I be then?"

"These are weighty problems, Joe," Mr. King said, and there was no disguising the twinkle in his eyes. "You could find yourself without a cook, and forced to live on sausage and eggs."

"... and wassail ..." Josh interjected.

"... for a long time." Mr. King cleared his throat. "Would you be willing to part with Abby?"

"Well, this is a consideration," Joe said.

Mary looked from Joe to Mrs. King, whose eyes were alert now.

"We would give her such a home, Mr. Shepard," the woman said. "I could certainly use the help, but more than that ..." She stopped, unable to continue.

Joe didn't seem to trust his voice, either, because he waited a long moment to continue. When he did, his voice sounded altered. "We could ask Abby what she thinks. Abby? Would you be willing to go home with the Kings?"

"You wouldn't be angry with me, would you?" Abby asked.

"Not a bit! We would miss you, but I look on this as an opportunity for you." Joe smiled at her. "I think you should do it."

Mr. King looked at his wife. "Myrtle?"

"Oh, yes, let us do this," Mrs. King said, her voice breathless, as if someone were hugging her tight. Her eyes clouded over for a moment. "Mr. King, I think we should return to Sheffield now, and forget Scarborough this year. I hope this does not disappoint you, but Abby must come first."

"I agree, Mrs. K," he replied. There was no disguising the relief in his voice, or the optimism.

Joe stood up. "I do have one condition: the three of you must return here for Christmas next year. I think we should make a tradition of it. What do you think, Mary?"

There he was, including her again. "I think it is a capital notion," she said.

"Then we all agree," Joe said. "Abby, Happy Christmas."

The Kings and Abby left when the dishes were done, their driver smiling so broadly that Mary thought his face would surely split. Abby hugged Joe for a long moment then whispered, "Mr. Shepard, I think you should go to the workhouse and ask for Sally Bawn. She cried and cried when you picked me in September."

"Sally Bawn, it is," he said. "I will tell her she comes highly recommended." He kissed her cheek and gave her a pat in the direction of the Kings. "That may be the wisest thing anyone ever did," he said to no one in particular as the post chaise rolled south. "Mary, it's your turn. Joshua, shall we take her to Muncie Farm?"

She blushed over the amount of luggage she had, but Joe got what he could into the spring wagon and assured her he would bring the rest tomorrow. Joshua climbed into the back, and he gave her a hand up onto the high seat. "Not exactly posh transportation," he said in apology. "I could probably hire a post chaise, but I'd rather not trouble the innkeeper on Christmas."

"I wouldn't have wanted that, either," she said, while he arranged a carriage robe over both of them. She knew she should keep it light, even though the familiar dread was returning. "After all, I am destined for a farm, and this will, in all likelihood, be the mode of transportation, will it not?"

Joe only smiled and spoke to the horses. She looked back at Joshua. "Are you entirely warm enough, my dear?" she asked.

He nodded, his eyes bright.

"I think it is awfully nice of Joshua to come along, especially when I suspect he wants to get back in your workshop," she told Joe.

"He likes Muncie Farm," Joe replied. The road was open, but narrow still with snow, and he concentrated on his driving.

Likes Muncie Farm? she asked herself. "He has been there before?" she asked.

"A time or two."

He was grinning now, and she wanted to ask him more, to pelt him with questions, but he appeared to be more interested in staying on his side of the road than talking. I will keep my counsel, she thought. He has been so obliging to put up with a houseful of unwanted guests, and I should not pester him.

They had traveled on the road to York not more than an hour, when he turned the horses west onto a lane that had been shoveled quite efficiently. "Do the road crews come out here, too?" she asked, surprised to see the road cleared.

"No. Muncie Farm is rather well organized."

She touched his shoulder and made him look at her when he started to chuckle. "Joe, are you practicing some great deception on me?"

He laughed out loud. "Just a little one, Mary, just a little one." He pointed with his whip. "There. Take a look at your grandmother's home." He grinned at her. "And resist the urge to smite me, please."

She looked; more than that, she stared, her mouth open. Located at the end of what by summer would probably be a handsome arch of trees, the farmhouse was a sturdy, three-storied manor of the fight gray stone common in the shire. The white shutters gleamed, and at each window she could see a flower box. The stone cornice over the double doors was even more imposing than the one Joe had commissioned for his house in Edgerly.

Barely able to contain himself, Joe pointed with his whip again. "See? Flower boxes already." He dodged when she made a motion to strike him with her reticule. "Be careful, Mary. I am the only parent Joshua has!"

"You are a scoundrel," she said with feeling. "You let me wallow in self-pity and ... and ... talk about learning to slop hogs and milk cows!"

He ducked again. "Do you have rocks in that reticule, my dear? I am certain that if you wished to slop the hogs, your grandmother would let you, although she might wonder why. Ow! Joshua, you could quit laughing and come to my defense!"

"You don't deserve any such consideration, sir!" she said, then stopped when the door opened. "Oh, my."

An older woman stood in the doorway. From her lace cap, to the Norwich shawl about her shoulders, to the cut of her dark dress, she was neat as a pin. Her back was straight, and she did not look much over sixty, if that. Mary looked closer, and then could not stop the tears that welled in her eyes. "Oh, Joe, I think I look a little like her," she whispered.

"You look a great deal like her," he whispered back, "but do you know, I didn't really see it until you mentioned Muncie Farm yesterday. Strange how that is."

Joe stopped the wagon in the well-graveled drive in front of the manor, leaped down, and held out his arms for her, his eyes bright with amusement. She sat there a moment more, watching as Joshua jumped from the back of the wagon and ran up the front steps. The woman hugged him, then kissed him and wished him Happy Christmas. "Your present is inside in the usual place, my dear," she told him, and stepped aside as he hurried into the house.

"I really don't understand what is going on," Mary said, completely mystified.

"I think we can make this clearer, if you will let me help you down, Mary," he said. This time there was compassion in his eyes. "Don't be afraid."

She did as he said. If she stood for a moment longer than necessary in the circle of his arms, she did not think he minded. He offered her his arm then, and they started up the short walk. "Mrs. Muncie, Happy Christmas to you!" he called. "I told you last week I would bring Josh over after Christmas dinner, but I have another guest. She was stranded at my house in all that snow, imagine that!" He stopped with her at the bottom of the steps. "May I introduce your granddaughter, Mary McIntyre?"

As Mary watched through a fog of her own, the woman began to cry. Mary released her death grip on Joe and ran up the steps. When the woman held out her arms, she rushed into them with a cry of her own. Mrs. Muncie's grip was surprisingly strong. As Mary clung to her, she saw in her mind's eye Abby clutched close to Mrs. King. Her heart spilled over with the sheer delight of coming home.

In another moment, Joe had his arms around both of them. "Ladies, do take your sensibilities inside. You know that Mr. Muncie would be growling about warming up the Great Plain of York, if he were still here." He shepherded them inside. In another moment, a maid had Mary's cloak in hand. Her bonnet already dangled down her back, relegated there by the tumult of her grandmother's greeting. She stood still, sniffing back her tears as Joseph untied the ribbon from her neck and handed the bonnet to the maid, who curtsied and rushed off, probably to spread the news that something amazing was happening in the sitting room.

The sitting room was as elegant as her own favorite morning room at Denton. Mary looked around in great appreciation, and then at Joe, who continued to grin at her. She sat next to her grandmother on the sofa and reached for her hand again.

"Mrs. Muncie, he let me believe that Muncie Farm was on the outer edges of barbarism. What a deceiver!"

"Yes, that is Joe," she agreed. She laughed, and then dabbed at her eyes with a lace handkerchief. "I tried to warn Melissa six years ago, but she thought he would do." She smiled at Joe, and blew him a kiss. "And he did."

Mary looked from one to the other. "I am beginning to suspect that an even greater deception has been practiced on me than I imagined! Will someone please tell me what is going on? Joshua, does your father run mad on a regular basis?"

From his spot on the floor where he had already opened his present—which looked like more tools—Joshua grinned at her. She felt her heart nearly stop as she took a closer look at him. "Oh, God," she whispered, and reached for Joe's hand, too. "Joe, don't tease me anymore. Is Josh ... oh, my stars ... is he my *nephew*?"

He squeezed her hand, then put his arm around her. "That he is, Mary. Melissa's first husband was Michael McIntyre, your mother's younger brother." He held up his free hand. "Don't look at me like that! I didn't know about the McIntyre name when I courted Melissa. It's common enough in these parts, and I didn't give it a thought when you were introduced to me as McIntyre." He touched her forehead with his own. "There were hard feelings about your mother running away, and Michael had told Melissa next to nothing." He looked at Mrs. Muncie. "He was younger, and he may not have known much. I never put your mother together with you until you mentioned Muncie Farm. And I can tell you don't believe me. Help me, Mrs. Muncie!"

The woman laughed and touched Mary's face. "Oh, my dear, he is a little innocent, or at least not as guilty as you would think. Yes, your name is McIntyre. I was married to Edward McIntyre, and had two children by him, Michael and Cynthia."

"Cynthia," Mary said. "In all this, no one ever told me her real name."

Mrs. Muncie closed her eyes for a moment. "Oh, my dear, all these years, all this sadness." She opened her eyes. "Cynthia was a lovely girl, and such a brilliant seamstress. I suppose there was something in her that none of us truly understood." She inclined her head toward Mary. "At any rate, when she was eighteen, and resisting a perfectly good marriage to a farmer, she and her father quarreled and she ran away." She held her handkerchief to her eyes again. "I cannot tell you how I grieved, but there was never a word from her."

"It is hard to take back harsh words," Mary murmured.

"It is," her grandmother agreed. "Edward McIntyre died two years after Cynthia ... left us. I ran the farm by myself for a while, and two years later married a neighbor, Stephen Muncie, who owned this wonderful place. He absorbed the McIntyre farm, and adopted Michael, because he had no children of his own."

"I only came into this district nine years ago, Mary, and I never knew Michael as a McIntyre," Joe said. "He was killed in a farming accident, and after a few years, I married his widow." He smiled. "And acquired Joshua, Melissa's son. Lord, this is strange! Mary, you have a grandmother and a nephew, which makes you Joshua's aunt, a closer relationship than I can claim with this lad I consider my own son." He shook his head. "We'll have to write the Kings and tell them about this."

And there you are, including me, Mary thought. I like it. Overwhelmed by the sheer pleasure of it all, she looked from Joe, to her grandmother, to Joshua, who had turned his attention back to his present. She released her grip on Joe and took Mrs. Muncie by the hand. "Grandmama, may I stay here with you?" she asked. "I do not think now that I would be happy anywhere else."

Mrs. Muncie embraced her. "This is your home." She held herself off from Mary to look at her. "In fact, it probably will belong to you and Joshua some day, considering that you are my heirs."

"I could even teach you how to milk," Joe teased. "Used to do a lot of that at Denton. Lord, wouldn't Thomas suffer palpitations if I actually mentioned that to anyone of his acquaintance!"

"What I expect you to do, dear sir, is find a way to come to terms with him," Mary said. She looked at Mrs. Muncie. "Let us here be your cautionary tale. Life is too short to foul it with petty discord."

"Your point is well taken," he admitted. He rose then, and motioned to Joshua. "Son, we had better go home before it gets too dark and the wolves start howling."

"Joe! Really!" Mrs. Muncie said. "Do you ever have a serious moment?"

"Plenty of them, madam," he replied, "but maybe not on Christmas. Mary, I promise to bring the rest of your numerous trunks tomorrow." He looked at Mrs. Muncie. "Do you want Joshua here for a couple of days?"

"Any time is fine with me ... with us ... Mrs. Muncie replied. She touched Mary's hand. "My dear, you will see much of Joshua in the spring, when his father makes the rounds of his clients in the shire. Josh always stays with me then."

As Mrs. Muncie summoned the housekeeper to make arrangements for Mary's room, Mary walked Joseph and Joshua to the door. "What can I say?" she asked as Joshua scrambled up into the high seat of the wagon.

Joseph hugged her. "Just forgive me for not spilling out my suspicions and realizations sooner, Mary."

"Sooner? Sooner?" she exclaimed. "You played that hand awfully close to your vest!"

He laughed and joined her nephew in the wagon. In another moment, they started down the lane. He looked back when they were near the end of the trees. On impulse, she blew him a kiss, then went up the steps and into the house again.

Mrs. Muncie was motioning to her on the stairs. She put

her arm around her grandmother and walked up the steps with her, and into a room easily as beautiful as her old room at Denton.

Mrs. Muncie touched the bedspread. "I made this for your mother when she was five years old," she said softly. She patted the pillow, then leaned against the mattress as though all her strength had left her. "When I first contacted Bow Street and told them to search for Cynthia McIntyre, I put this back on the bed. Oh, Mary, welcome home."

Her heart full, Mary hugged her grandmother. "Happy Christmas, my dear," she whispered.

She didn't want the embrace to end, but her grandmother started to chuckle. "Oh, my dear," she said finally, "you should be looking out the window right now from my vantage point. Better still, I think you should hurry down the stairs."

Mary opened her eyes and turned around to see what was causing Mrs. Muncie so much amusement. "Why is he coming back?" she asked, and then she knew with all her heart just why. "Oh, excuse me," she said as she started for the door.

"Here. Take my shawl. It's December, remember, my dear?"

She snatched up her grandmother's shawl and swirled it around her shoulders as she hurried down the stairs. She flung open the door, then closed it quickly, remembering the late Mr. Muncie's admonition about heating all of Yorkshire. Joe was out of the wagon seat, and she was in his arms before she had time to clear the last step. With a shaky laugh, he took her down the last step and held her off from him for a moment.

"I'm perfectly sober, Mary McIntyre," he warned her. "I'm really going to mean it this time. Did you just blow me a kiss?"

"Only because you were too far away," she replied. It must have been the right answer, because he kissed her soundly, thoroughly, and completely at her grandmother's front door. He held her close then, and she wrapped Mrs. Muncie's shawl around both of them.

"Poor Mrs. Muncie," he murmured in her ear. "I mean, what kind of a common scoundrel and skirt raiser would take away her granddaughter so soon?"

"You would, my love," she whispered.

Bryner Photography

A WELL-KNOWN VETERAN OF the romance writing field, Carla Kelly is the author of thirty-one novels and three non-fiction works, as well as numerous short stories and articles for various publications. She is the recipient of two RITA Awards from Romance Writers of America for Best Regency of the Year; two Spur Awards from Western Writers of America; two Whitney Awards, one for Best Romance Fiction, 2011, and one for Best Historical Fiction, 2012; and a Lifetime Achievement Award from *Romantic Times*.

Carla's interest in historical fiction is a byproduct of her lifelong study of history. She has a BA in Latin American

History from Brigham Young University and an MA in Indian Wars History from University of Louisiana-Monroe. She's held a variety of jobs, including public relations work for major hospitals and hospices, feature writer and columnist for a North Dakota daily newspaper, and ranger in the National Park Service (her favorite job) at Fort Laramie National Historic Site and Fort Union Trading Post National Historic Site. She has worked for the North Dakota Historical Society as a contract researcher. Interest in the Napoleonic Wars at sea led to a recent series of novels about the British Channel Fleet during that conflict.

Of late, Carla has written two novels set in southeast Wyoming in 1910 that focus on her Mormon background and her interest in ranching.

You can find Carla on the Web at:

www.carlakellyauthor.com.

CAMEL PRESS

The All-New Spanish Brand Series

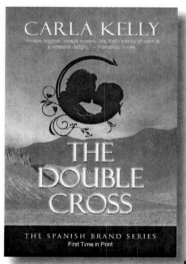

At the end of the 18th Century, during the decline of the Spanish Empire in the New World, a brand inspector saves a lovely orphan from her cruel relatives and sets out to solve the mystery of her lost inheritance.

Marco and Paloma fight the scourge of smallpox by bravely venturing onto the Staked Plains, stronghold of the Comanche. As part of a devil's bargain, they must put themselves at the mercy of these dangerous enemies and try to inoculate them.

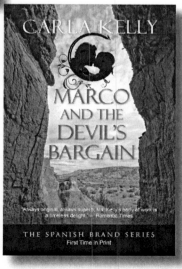

Carla Kelly's First Novel

CARLA KELLY

DAUGHTER OF FORTUNE

Two-time Rita Award winner for
Best Regency Romance and recipient of a
Romantic Times Career Achievement Award.

Maria Espinosa is "La Afortunata." First she survives
the 1679 cholera epidemic in Mexico City, then
an Apache raid on the caravan transporting her to
Santa Fe. Rejected by her sister, Maria goes to live
with a ranching family living uneasily among the
Pueblos and inspires a rivalry between Diego and
his half-Indian brother Cristobal. When the Indians
revolt, will Maria's good fortune hold?

Other Camel Press Editions of Regency Romances by Carla Kelly

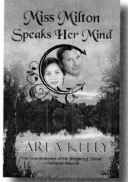

CPSIA information can be obtained at www.ICGtesting.com
Printed in the USA
LVOW07s1211101214

418149LV00005B/342/P